Trial
by
Sorcery

Dragon Riders of Osnen Book 1

RICHARD FIERCE

Dragonfire Press

Cover design by germancreative.

Cover art by Rosauro Ugang

ISBN: 978-1-947329-25-6

CONTENTS

MAP

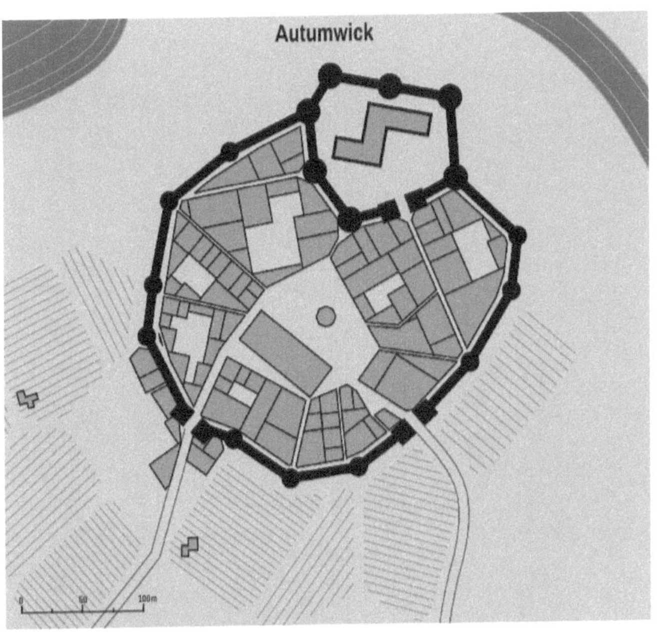

1

I marveled at the vastness of the Citadel.

It was home to the Dragon Guard, the greatest warriors of the kingdom. While that was impressive alone, it was made even more amazing because it was also the home of dragons. The massive, powerful creatures were kept in the lower chamber of the castle. At least, that's what my father used to tell me.

A wall forty feet high surrounded the city of Autumnwick, as well as the stone fortress that towered behind it. This was my first time seeing the place, and it was just as large and imposing as I'd always imagined it to be. The massive gates that provided entrance through the wall were manned with guards armed to the teeth. A small line had formed at the entrance as the guards checked everyone entering.

I traveled downhill and joined the line, adjusting my sword belt. The weight of the blade continuously pulled down on my pants. It made me reconsider my decision to use a side sheath instead of one that went over the shoulder. It was too late to change my mind now. I'd spent the last of my coins to reach the Citadel, and I doubted the school would allow me to carry a blade during my training anyway.

The line shuffled forward slowly. I did my best

to remain patient, but it was difficult. I was finally here! The home of the Dragon Guard! I'd dreamed of joining their ranks for as long as I could remember. My father's stories had always been filled with awe and wonder as he described his dragon and the bond they shared.

Although it was still early in the day, the sky was clear and the sun beat down mercilessly. I could feel droplets of sweat running down my back and sides. I drank the last of the water in my canteen and continued to wait. After what felt like an eternity of baking in the sun, I was next for inspection. I glanced behind me and saw the line was much longer now. There were at least a hundred people waiting to get into the city.

"Hold it there, low born," one of the guards said.

I looked ahead, thinking he was speaking to me. He wasn't. His attention was on a girl in front of me with long black hair. They'd already given her sack a thorough check, but the one talking grabbed her by the elbow and pulled her aside. I couldn't hear what he was saying to her because he'd lowered his voice, but whatever it was, the girl did not look amused.

"You, stop gawking and get over here."

The other guard was glaring at me. I hurried forward. The guard looked me up and down and frowned.

"What's your business?" he asked.

"I'm here to sign up for the school," I answered, trying to ignore the sweat sliding down my back. The other guard was still speaking with the girl, and he was being a little too touchy in my opinion.

"Another low born seeking fame and riches, huh?"

The guard was wearing a helm, but the ends of his hair sticking out from under it were blond. He was a high born, a noble. They were all the same. They thought they were better than everyone else simply because they were born with a different shade of hair color. I'd been bullied in my hometown a few times, not just for my social standing, and I knew in a city this size that it would be much worse.

The problem with this guard, however, was that he was only paying attention to my hair. He clearly didn't notice the insignia that was sewn into my upper sleeve. I didn't like to flounce it, but sometimes it was fun to bring a noble down a peg or two.

"Stop it," the girl with the other guard shouted. He'd pulled her close and was trying to kiss her. I'd seen enough. I turned my body so that the guard could see my insignia and smiled at him. His eyes widened for a brief moment, then he collected himself and waved me through.

"Apologies," he muttered.

I nodded at him, still smiling, and walked over to where the other guard was harassing the girl.

"Is there a problem, cousin?" I asked.

Both the girl and the guard looked at me. The girl was confused and the guard looked irritated.

"I figured you would have been lost in the market by now," I said to the girl. I was hoping she would catch on to what I was doing and play along. She tilted her head ever so slightly as a wordless sign of thanks and stepped back from the guard.

"I'm fine," she huffed. "This gentleman was just telling me how to get to the school."

"How kind of you, sir," I said, showing off my insignia to him as well. He looked at it, then looked me in the eyes. He hated that he couldn't stop me. I could see the seething anger in his blue eyes.

"Would you mind repeating the directions? My cousin is terrible at remembering things like that. Aren't you, cousin?"

I exchanged glances with the girl. She shrugged. "What can I say? I'm not used to doing things on my own."

The guard glowered at me. Through clenched teeth, he said, "Go straight. Through the market. When you reach the wall, turn right. The entrance is on the left."

Before I could antagonize him further, he stomped past me and returned to his post with the other guard.

"A bit of a jerk, that one," I said. The girl was already through the gate, leaving me talking to myself. I followed her and had to walk twice as fast to catch up.

"I'm Eldwin," I said.

"Go away," the girl replied.

"I'm sorry, I thought I just helped you back there."

The girl stopped and turned around, placing her hands on her hips and giving me a death stare.

"Did I ask for your help?"

"No …"

"Do I look like some sort of helpless wench that needs rescue?" she demanded.

"Uh, no …"

"That's because I'm not," she growled. "I can take care of myself."

"Sorry," I said lamely, putting my hands up. Her eyes widened slightly at the sight of my right hand. "I didn't mean to upset you. I just thought … never mind. Forget that I said or did anything."

I walked past her and continued following the road. The girl's response to seeing my mangled hand was the same as everyone else who saw it. Horror, disgust, you name it. It came as no surprise to me anymore.

The buildings on either side were short and squat, all of them built with a dull gray stone. The buildings on the right ended after several feet and opened into a large space filled with vendors.

Multicolored tents were arranged in orderly rows and delicious scents filled the air, making my mouth water. My stomach growled and I absently patted it.

My breakfast had been filling, but I'd walked the last few miles to Autumnwick and now I was hungry. Considering I didn't have any money for food, I was hoping the school would provide meals. My father had never told me about his training days, so I wasn't sure what awaited me.

All the sights and smells temporarily distracted my mind from the girl, who I found to be quite pretty. Her attitude, on the other hand, made me question my judgment. I watched the various vendors as they stood under their tents, hawking their wares and trying to negotiate prices with potential customers. The sun seemed to grow hotter by the second as I stood there. I wiped the back of my hand across my forehead and was about to continue to the school when the girl walked up to me.

"I'm sorry," she huffed.

"Don't worry about it," I said.

"No, really. I didn't mean to be rude. It's just …" she trailed off and looked down. "My whole life, people have tried to help me for their own gain. I've made it a point in my life to never need help from anyone."

What she said didn't make any sense. She was a low born like me, so what would anyone have to gain by helping her? I pushed the thought away.

"Apology accepted," I said. "I didn't mean to offend you or anything. I thought that guard was being a little forceful for his own good and thought I could help diffuse the situation."

"Thank you," she said. She paused a moment, then said, "I'm Maren."

Maren. That was different … but beautiful.

"Nice to meet you, Maren," I said. "Are you really going to the school?"

"I am," Maren confirmed. "I want to be a Dragon Guard."

"So do I," I said. "My father was one."

"Was?"

"He died," I answered. "In a big battle ten years ago."

Maren's eyed widened. "Wait. Your father was Matthias Baines?"

I nodded. "That's how I got this," I pointed to the insignia on my sleeve. "Noble by Deed."

She stared at the patch intently for a moment, then turned toward the market. "Something smells good," she said. "Want to help me find what it is?"

I wanted to say yes, but because I didn't have any money, I was forced to decline. Thankfully, she didn't ask for a reason. I wouldn't have lied to her if she had, but I would have been embarrassed. My father's heroics may have earned my family a noble title, but that title didn't come with riches.

"I'll see you at the school," I said.

Maren shrugged and disappeared into the crowded marketplace. A droplet of sweat threatened to drip into my eye and I wiped it away, then continued toward the Citadel.

Girls were odd creatures.

2

The entrance to the Citadel was much more heavily guarded than the city gates. And these guards weren't the city guard, either. They were Dragon Guards. Their armor was decorated to look like dragon scales, but it was versatile and practical for battle. Behind the assemblage of guards was a long wooden table that had weapons scattered haphazardly on its surface.

As I drew nearer, there was a *whooshing* sound that echoed off the massive walls and made the items on the table clatter. The guards seemed unperturbed by the noise, but I was trying to figure out what it was and where it was coming from. Suddenly, a massive blue dragon swooped down from the sky and landed in the courtyard.

I held my breath in awe as I stared at the powerful beast. It was easily thirty feet long from its nose to its tail. The dragon's rider slid off the beast's back from the shoulder and landed on the ground gracefully. I snapped my mouth closed and blinked several times. In all the years my father had been a dragoon, I never had the chance to see his dragon. Aside from when the guards traveled the kingdom, dragons were to be kept at the Citadel under lock and key. I didn't know why, though.

Now that I was standing before a dragon, I could hardly fathom how big it was. Its shoulder was six feet above the ground and its wingspan was massive. I tried to eyeball the length, but it had to be almost a hundred feet across. My focus on the dragon was broken as the guards got my attention.

"Hey there," one of them called out. "Step forward."

I did as he asked and walked closer, but my gaze remained locked on the dragon. An older man approached the creature and took its reins, then led it around the back of the castle. With a swish of its tail, the dragon disappeared behind the fortress and I looked at the guard who'd spoken.

"First time, huh?" he grinned. "I remember my first time seeing a dragon, too. It's something you never forget."

"I had no idea they were so large," I said.

"Yeah, they're impressive, all right. That one was full-grown, but blues aren't even the largest dragons."

"There are dragons bigger than that one?" I asked.

The guard nodded, still grinning. "Anyway, I assume you're here to sign up for admission?"

"Yes," I replied.

"We've got a big crowd this year. We can't take everyone, but the best of luck to you."

"Thank you. Do I need to check my sword?" I asked, eyeing the table behind him.

"Yes. We'll take the weapons to the armory and catalog them to the appropriate students. Once you're accepted as an apprentice, or rejected, you'll get the weapon back."

I hesitantly unstrapped the weapon from around my waist and offered it to the guard. He noticed my uneasiness.

"Don't worry, we'll keep it safe."

"I don't doubt that," I said. "It's just … it was my father's."

The guard pulled the blade a few inches from the scabbard and read the inscription on the blade, then looked at me with interest.

"You're Matthias's son?"

I nodded proudly. "Did you know my father?"

"No, but I saw him around here a few times. He's a hero, you know?"

"I know."

"I know your surname, but what's your given name?"

"Eldwin," I said.

The guard nodded slowly and set the weapon on the table with what seemed like reverence. He wrote down my name on a parchment, along with a description of my blade. I waited expectantly for the guard to say something after he finished, but he remained silent.

"Do I just go in?" I asked.

The guard seemed confused. "Do you not know what to do?" he asked.

I shook my head.

"Ah, my apologies. You'll go through the main doors there," he pointed an armored hand toward the front of the Citadel. "The Administrators will sign you in and tell you where your room is. The ceremonies don't start for a few more hours, but you can get some food from the dining hall if you're hungry. Don't eat too much, though. The stuff they serve at the ceremony is top-notch."

"Thank you," I said. "It was nice talking to you."

I joined a small group of people who were heading for the Citadel's entrance and listened to their excited conversations. Two of them were nobles by birth, both blond-headed. They were talking about their lavish trips to the Citadel and the disappearance of the princess. That was news to me. The king's daughter was missing? I could envision legions of dragon riders scouring the kingdom for her.

Three low borns were talking about all the amazing things they had seen in the market. That brought Maren to mind again and I glanced over my shoulder to see if she had entered the courtyard yet, but I didn't see her. I stayed at the back of the group and kept my mangled right hand as concealed as I could. A short stairway led to the large oak doors that towered as tall as four men stacked atop one another.

As I stepped inside, an unmistakable calmness draped over everyone. The excited conversations of my peers died. We all stood in the doorway, staring around the enormous hall. Marble columns were spaced every ten feet and supported the domed ceiling above. People dressed in flowing robes were moving in every direction, their steps quiet but purposeful. I couldn't tell the difference between their ranks, though I knew there were a few different posts within the school hierarchy.

"Name?"

The question broke the silence and I snapped my gaze to the right to find a tall, elderly man standing behind a lectern. Atop the lectern was a book and quill. His robes were brown, plain and unadorned.

"Speak up, boy, I can't hear you."

One of the nobles leaned toward the old man and repeated his name so loud it echoed off the walls. His name was Simon. I didn't catch his surname. The robed man dipped his quill into an inkwell and then wrote the name down, then told Simon what room he would be staying in. The process continued through all my peers until I was last.

"Name?" the old man asked.

"Eldwin Baines," I answered.

The man peered down at me and smiled. "Yes, I should have seen the resemblance. My eyes aren't what they used to be." He scribbled my name down in his book and then said, "You'll be staying in the North Wing, second floor, third room."

"I'm sorry, but where is that?" I asked.

"Don't worry about that right now," the man said. "You'll meet your Curate at the ceremony later and they will show you to your wing, as well as explain the rules of the school."

I nodded. "The soldier outside said we could get some food from the dining hall?"

"Yes, that's correct. The dining hall is in the South Wing."

A robed woman was walking past and the old man held up a hand. The woman paused and the man gestured toward me.

"Surrel, would you be a dear and show Eldwin here to the dining hall?"

"Of course, Provost," Surrel replied. She looked at me and smiled. "Follow me."

I fell into step behind the woman and glanced back at the elder. A new group had entered the hall and he began taking their names. He seemed nice. And apparently, he knew my father. Surrel led me down long, quiet hallways and eventually we turned a corner and the sweet smell of freshly baked bread drifted on the air.

"The door to the left is the dining hall," Surrel said. "You can stay in there until the ceremony if you want. Although the Provost has assigned you a room, you won't be allowed to enter it until your Curate has outlined the school's rules."

"Do I have to stay in there?" I asked.

"No, of course not. Feel free to wander the academy. The gardens outside are my particular favorite."

"Thank you for bringing me here," I said.

"You're welcome."

With a slight bow of her head, Surrel left back the way we'd come and I entered the dining hall. Like the market, a swirl of different scents assailed my senses and I knew it would be hard to keep from eating more than I should with the ceremony later. I joined a line of students and grabbed a tray from one of the stacks.

As we slowly walked forward, a long wooden bar was covered with various foods. Freshly baked bread, cheese wheels, steaming mutton, baked turkey … it was more food in one place than I had ever seen. I took a little bit of everything and by the time I reached the end of the bar, my tray was full.

I spotted an empty table and sat down, then glanced around at the other students. Everyone was focused on eating or talking. The two nobles I had seen earlier were sitting together. If they were like other nobles I had met, they probably saw themselves as better than everyone else and wouldn't be caught dead talking to a low born like me.

Disappointed, I cast a final glance around the room and began eating. The flavors that hit my tongue were delicious. I'd always loved my mother's cooking, but this school's food put her to shame. The spices from the meats set my tongue aflame, but thankfully there was a pitcher of water at every table. I poured myself some and took a long drink, swishing the cool water around in my mouth to ease the burning. It wasn't overwhelming, but I had never grown accustomed to spicy food. I was the oddity of my family.

By the time I'd cleared half the tray, I slowly became aware that the general sound of the dining hall had grown quiet. I looked around and noticed that several students were looking in my direction. I turned the other way, but I didn't see anything that would have drawn their attention.

And then it hit me.

I was using my mangled hand to eat with. The other students were staring at *me*.

3

"A cripple thinks he'll be able to ride a dragon?"

Despite the many times I'd heard similar things hurled in my direction, the words stung me emotionally. I swallowed the food in my mouth and took a drink, then turned to see who said it. One of the nobles, the one named Simon, was smirking at me.

I thought about just ignoring him, but for some reason I couldn't explain, I decided to confront him.

"What was that?" I asked.

Simon's smile grew larger and he popped a grape into his mouth.

"I said, a cripple thinks he'll be able to ride a dragon."

"Who said I was a cripple?"

"Look at your hand, low born. It's as mangled as a dragon's toy. How would you hold the reigns? And what about wielding a blade? How would you fight on the back of a dragon?"

The hall had gone silent as Simon spoke, and all eyes were on me.

"I can wield a blade just fine," I replied. "And I'll learn to hold the reigns."

"Oh? Prove that you can hold a sword," Simon

said. "Challenge me to a duel."

Just as I was going to respond, a familiar voice spoke.

"Such unbecoming speech from a noble. And even worse, from someone who thinks they are worthy of something simply because they were born with a different shade of hair color."

It was Maren. She stood a few feet away from Simon, arms folded across her chest. Her black hair spiraled down her shoulders. Though she was a low born like me, she was very imposing at the moment.

Simon was also taken aback momentarily, but he stood up and glared at her.

"How dare you speak to me like that, low born!"

"I should say the same to you, considering Eldwin here is a Noble by Deed."

Simon looked at me and I flashed the insignia on my shoulder to him. His face reddened and he opened his mouth to say something but stormed out of the dining hall instead. The other noble got up and left as well. Maren came over to my table and sat down.

"I could have handled it," I said. "You know you just made an enemy, right?"

Maren shrugged. "I've been surrounded by enemies my entire life. What's one more?"

There she went, saying something that didn't make any sense. As low borns, we were the lowest in society, but we weren't surrounded by enemies. I ignored her comment. My throat had gone dry and I drank some more water.

"You hungry?" I asked.

"No. I ate in the market. I found that delicious smell. It tasted even better."

"What was it?"

Maren shrugged. "Some exotic meat. I've never heard of it. How's the food here?"

"Delicious," I replied. "Probably the best food I've ever had."

"You don't get out much, do you?" Maren laughed.

"What do you mean?"

"Nothing." She waved a hand dismissively. "There's a few hours before the ceremony. Any plans?"

"No?" I said, then took a bite out of the bread on my tray. It was light and fluffy.

"Good. You can come with me."

I finished chewing and asked, "Where?"

Maren leaned forward and lowered her voice to a whisper. "To see the dragons."

"What?" My heart fell from my chest into my stomach. We couldn't just go wandering into the dragon stables! Or could we? I washed the bread down with some water and lowered my voice. "Are we allowed to see them? We're not even sworn in yet."

The smile on Maren's face told me everything I needed to know. She was a troublemaker. I leaned back in my chair and frowned at her.

"I don't want to be kicked out of the school. I *can't* be."

"You won't get kicked out," Maren chided. "If anything, we'll be forced to clean the dishes or something like that. As you said, we've not been sworn in yet. How can they kick us out if we aren't part of the student body yet?"

I knew it was stupid, but her logic had a ring to it that I couldn't deny. I stared at her in silence, wanting to tell her no, planning to end this insanity immediately. When I spoke, I found myself agreeing to go with her. I pondered how that happened as I followed her down the long hallways, passing robed students and teachers alike.

"Have you been here before?" I asked. She walked with confidence as if she'd walked these halls a hundred times.

"No. I've seen maps of the school, though."

Maren had memorized maps of the place? I shook my head. She was lying. Maybe she was some third- or fourth-year student pretending to be new and only wanted to get me into trouble? I was about to turn back when we reached a small wooden door that was relatively hidden by the shadows. If she hadn't stopped at it, I would have walked right past without noticing it.

"Here," she said softly, but her voice carried

along the hallway. "This is a door used by the servants. It leads outside near the entrance to the stables."

I have to admit, I was afraid. The risk of being caught and kicked out of the Citadel was something I didn't want to chance, but the idea that dragons were just outside that door was too tempting.

"Let's go," I said.

Maren nodded, that blasted smile on her face. She twisted the handle and pushed the door open. A wave of heat washed over me. Although I knew it had only been a short time since I'd entered the Citadel, it had felt like days had passed. The sun was still high in the sky and it beat down mercilessly. Maren led the way and I followed closely behind her. About fifty paces to the left was the large opening of a cave that led below ground, a massive burrow beneath the Citadel that served as the stables.

"There are two guards a few feet inside," Maren whispered over her shoulder. "We'll need to sneak past them."

Guards? Oh, great. My doubt began to gnaw at me again. "Maybe we shouldn't do this," I said. "We should wait until it's officially time for us to see them."

Maren turned to look at me. "Are you a chicken?" she asked. "All I'm hearing is you balking."

Despite my fear, that made me laugh and I

snorted. Maren winked at me and turned back around.

"They're playing dice," she said. "Don't drag your feet and we should be able to get by without them noticing."

We slipped into the shade of the cave's entrance and my eyes slowly adjusted to the gloom. Maren was right. The two guards were sitting cross-legged on the ground and they were taking turns dumping dice out of a wooden cup.

As we slinked past the guards and continued lower underground, the air became cooler. It was pitch black for fifty feet or so, then everything was illuminated by torches that lined the walls on either side. Spaced intermittently on either side were smaller caves, though they were still vast in size.

I glanced into one and saw giant eyes glittering in the darkness. I'm certain my heart skipped a beat and I was distantly aware of Maren talking, but I couldn't make out the words. The massive outline of a dragon's head moved toward me and I could smell something acrid in the air. My legs went stiff. I was frozen in place, too afraid to move. The dragon drew nearer and inhaled through its nostrils.

My clothes fluttered from the pull of the air and the dragon snorted once, then opened its maw. I was going to die. There was no doubt in my mind as I saw the razor-sharp teeth of the beast. Then the dragon made a choking sound and before I could force my legs to move, a foul-smelling mucus flew forth from the dragon's mouth and splattered all over me.

Disbelief alone kept me from vomiting. The dragon backed away and disappeared back into the shadows of its cave. I turned to look at Maren. Her eyes were wide, her mouth agape. I thought for sure she was going to start laughing at me, but she didn't.

"What is this?" I asked lowly, horrified.

"I think it's dragon phlegm," Maren replied.

"I'm trying not to freak out," I said.

"At least it's not acid. Then you'd be dead."

Now she started laughing. I did, too. I had forgotten all about the guards until I heard their boots cracking along the floor as their silhouettes came into view.

"Come on, this way!" Maren said. She grabbed my hand and pulled me along behind her. I nearly slipped in the puddle of phlegm on the floor, but thankfully I kept my balance. We ran further into the cave, going deeper into the darkness until there were no sputtering torches on the walls. The blackness was absolute, and Maren slowed her pace. She continued to hold my hand as we walked. I convinced myself it was only because she didn't want to lose me in the darkness.

"Where are we going?" I whispered.

"Away from the guards," Maren replied.

I rolled my eyes. "Yeah, I know that. I mean, where exactly are we going? The exit is behind us."

"There is always more than one way into a place," Maren said. "Considering who your father was, I'm surprised you don't know more about the school. Or dragons."

She was right. My father had never really talked about the school or the things he did as a dragoon in detail. I had always assumed he wanted to keep that part of his life separate from the rest so that he could have some semblance of normalcy.

"Stop," Maren said. "I think it's right around here."

"What is?" "I asked.

"The secret door," Maren said. "I need you to lift me."

"How exactly?"

"Just put your hands together so I can use them as a step."

I bit my lower lip. She clearly had forgotten about my hand. I cleared my throat.

"Yeah, that's not going to work. I'll have to wrap my arms around your waist and lift you that way."

"That should work," Maren replied. "Just don't get any ideas."

I snorted in reply and bent down slightly, then wrapped my arms around her midsection and lifted her.

"Higher," she said. "I can't reach the ceiling."

Maren wasn't heavy but trying to lift her higher was a little awkward. I grunted as I bounced upward and readjusted my arms a little lower. Her thighs pressed against my head and despite her warning, I couldn't stop the flow of inappropriate thoughts that spun around in my mind. She made noises as she stretched to reach the ceiling, which didn't help at all.

A moment later, there was a brief screeching sound. Light from above filtered down into the cave around us and Maren pulled herself up through a manhole. She offered her hand to me and I jumped a few times, but I couldn't reach her. She disappeared for a few seconds, then reappeared and dropped a rope down.

"Try this," she said.

I grabbed ahold of the rope and climbed up. The manhole opened into a plain stone chamber. I laid on the floor beside her, most of the dragon phlegm still wet against my skin. I frowned in disgust.

"Where are we?" I asked.

Maren giggled in response. "The women's bath chamber."

4

A few hours later, after I had cleaned the dragon phlegm off and washed my clothes, I sat in the school's temple with the other hopefuls. There were roughly a hundred of us and the building was a cacophony of voices.

Maren had left me alone when we escaped the women's bathing room, and thankfully the mens hadn't been too far away. I was able to get away with at least some shred of my dignity. To her credit, Maren hadn't said anything about my dragon encounter other than she'd never heard of anything like that happening before.

Neither had I, but what did either one of us know about dragons? Not much. I looked around the room and spotted Maren a few pews over. The temple's layout was simple. Rows of pews on the left and right, divided by a walkway down the middle, and an upraised dais at the front. Large stained-glass windows behind the dais portrayed a dragoon riding a massive red dragon. I knew that dragons had different colors, but I didn't know how many there were. I'd seen a blue one earlier, and there was a red one on the glass. My thoughts were interrupted when the school's master called for attention.

I craned my neck to see around the person in front of me and saw the master was tall and thin. His age was indeterminate to me. He was at least in his sixties, but I only thought that because his hair was entirely gray, including the short beard that clothed his chin. I didn't think I would be able to hear him from where I was sitting, but his voice boomed across the entire room.

"Good evening, everyone. Welcome to the Citadel. I am Master Pevus, head of the school. This is our largest group of hopefuls in many years. Let us hope that this is just the beginning of changing times."

Master Pevus shuffled around the platform and looked out at us, peering in every direction before nodding to himself. That was odd. Was he looking for someone?

"As many of you probably already know, we do not accept every potential student, even if they pass the three tests. The reason for this is not for you to know. Suffice it to say that there are things here that will remain a mystery, no matter how many years you devote to your studies."

He inhaled a deep breath and tightened his grip on his wooden staff. I tilted my head curiously. That staff hadn't been there before. Or had it? I blinked and looked at the person next to me, but if they were aware of the same thing, they didn't show it. I turned my attention back to Pevus.

"The servants are setting up the feast and we will all move to the dining hall in the next few moments. Please wait until they have finished laying everything out before you start partaking of it."

Master Pevus turned his head and cleared his throat, then continued speaking. "I've heard the whispered rumors going around about the new color of dragon that will be in the bonding ceremony."

At this, muted conversations sprung to life around me. Master Pevus raised a hand for silence.

"I can confirm those rumors are true. We typically have reds, greens, and blues, but this year we will see a few black dragons in the mix. It has been a long time since we've had black dragons, so we have brought in a teacher who will aid in your training should a black dragon choose to bond with you."

I tried to picture what a black dragon would look like, but considering I'd only seen one dragon, my imagination fell flat. He had just named off four colors, though, and that seemed like a lot to me. Of course, I was completely uneducated about dragons, so I was probably wrong. Maybe there were hundreds of different colors.

"Those of you familiar with the Citadel may notice some recent changes around the grounds. To alleviate the questions directed to your Curates, just refer yourselves back to my original statement about mysteries. If you annoy your Curate with unnecessary questions, you'll find yourself cleaning dishes or some other unsavory task."

I made a mental note to remember that. The last thing I wanted to do was get punished. After all, I had to live up to my father's respected memory. Master Pevus walked slowly down the center aisle and glanced up and down the rows of pews.

"I will lead the way to the dining hall. Beginning with the last row, you shall follow behind me. Once everyone from the row has fallen into line, the next row will do the same. Repeat this for every row."

I turned around to watch Master Pevus lead the way. As he commanded, everyone rose from the pews and got in line, following him to the dining hall. My row was ahead of Maren's, so I didn't get to talk with her much as we walked. There were whispered conversations around me. I eavesdropped on a few of them and learned that people on the border of Osnen were reporting strange things.

One conversation, between two young girls, revealed that rumors were being spread about the return of the someone called the False King. I didn't know who that was, but I listened intently anyway. Apparently, everyone thought he had died years ago.

The rest of the conversations were boring. I was surprised when someone poked me in the back and I glanced over my shoulder to see it was Maren.

"Where'd you come from?" I asked.

"My mother and the authorities are still trying to determine that."

She said it with such a straight face that for a second, I actually believed her. Maren's face broke into a smile and she giggled. "I'm kidding, Eldwin. Has anyone told you that you're too gullible?"

"You would be the first, actually," I replied. "And I'm not gullible."

"Right." Maren offered me an exaggerated wink.

We reached the dining hall and my eyes widened as we entered. The room looked completely different from what it had just a few hours earlier. The tables had been rearranged and a stage had been erected in the back corner. A troop of performers was standing off to the side, talking among themselves. Master Pevus stood patiently near the doors. He waited until everyone had entered before speaking.

"You have all been assigned a Curate based on your housing assignment. Each table has been labeled with the wing and floor numbers. Please find your tables and take a seat."

That caused some chaos as a hundred of us tried to navigate between the maze of tables to find where we belonged. A lot of unintentional pushing occurred, but eventually, everyone found their tables and sat down. I looked around at the others at my table and was surprised to find Maren and Simon were assigned to the same Curate I was. Obviously, I was happy about the first and disappointed by the second.

Servants rushed to finish placing food on the tables and once they had cleared the room, Master Pevus tapped his staff on the floor for attention.

"Before we eat, I'd like to introduce you all to your leaders. Curates, if you would?"

A group of robed men and women entered the dining hall and separated, each one standing next to a table. Our Curate was a man. He was middle-aged, with short brown hair and a clean-shaven face. His eyes were green and he had the whitest teeth I had ever seen.

"Greetings," he said. "I am Curate Anesko. Once dinner is finished, I'll lead you to your rooms and explain the rules of the school. There aren't many, but they are important and in place for good reason. Enjoy the meal and the ceremony, for tomorrow begins the most difficult journey you've ever experienced."

I exchanged looks with Maren. She shrugged and began filling her plate. I wasn't very hungry, so I picked a few delicious looking items and ate sparingly. I knew I shouldn't have eaten as much as I did earlier, but I couldn't help it. I was parched and drank several cups of water. Before long, I could feel my bladder starting to cry out at me. I had no idea where I could relieve myself, so I tried to ignore my body by bouncing my leg beneath the table.

While I was looking around the room and trying not to piss myself, I noticed a red-faced man enter the dining hall. He seemed flustered and approached Master Pevus. They shared a whispered discussion and Master Pevus's face seemed troubled. The messenger left and Master Pevus looked directly at me. I swallowed hard. Did he know about my earlier transgression with the dragon?

That intensified my need to relieve myself, but

as the night continued on, he never said anything to me. Perhaps it was just my wild imagination. The performers entertained us with feats of acrobatics, juggling, and many other acts. Eventually, I found myself yawning and the need to empty my bladder was too strong. I rose from the table and approached Curate Anesko.

"Where are the lavatories from here?" I asked. My body was starting to get hot and sweaty.

I was certain he could see my discomfort. Curate Anesko motioned me to follow him and led me out of the dining hall. We went to the left and at the end of the hall, turned right. The mens bathing room that I had used earlier was on the right. I thanked the Curate and quickly relieved myself, breathing a sigh of relief.

"Tell your friend to watch her back," a quiet voice said.

I turned to look, startled, but nobody was there.

5

After the ceremony was over, we followed Curate Anesko to the North Wing. A large staircase led up to the second floor and we all stood at the bottom. I'd forgotten which room the Provost had assigned me to. It seemed everyone else had as well.

The Curate ended up having to tell us which rooms to go to. I had assumed that we all had our own rooms, and was sorely disappointed when I realized that it was two students to every room. And of course, my roommate was Simon.

Before we were allowed to turn in for the night, Anesko demanded our undivided attention. We lined up single file, facing the Curate. He clasped his hands behind his back and slowly looked down the line of students, pausing a few seconds as he reached each of us.

"There are a few rules that you need to observe. It is of the utmost importance that you do not break these rules, or your time here will be *very* short."

Anesko's gaze lingered on me for some reason, and again I wondered if Maren and I had been seen by someone earlier. The Curate continued his speech, his stern gaze looking over everyone as if we were all criminals.

"Firstly, no one is allowed out of their room after curfew, which is the third bell after dinner.

The bell rings every hour on the hour from dawn until curfew. If you are caught gallivanting around the grounds other than to use the lavatory, you will answer to me. Is that understood?"

We all nodded mutely.

"Good. Secondly, during the hours outside of curfew, you are allowed anywhere on the grounds except the dragon stables. Until you are promoted to the rank of Adept, you might be lucky enough to glimpse a dragon in passing. Dragons are powerful and cunning creatures, and until you've mastered the skills necessary to keep from falling under their power, you will *not* get within fifty feet of one. Is that also understood?"

I swallowed hard and nodded, remembering how the dragon earlier had only been a few feet away. Not only could the dragon have eaten me, but it seemed that they had powers? Were they able to use magic like sorcerers? I knew that a dragoon and a dragon had a special bond, but apart from that small knowledge, my father hadn't told me much more.

"Thirdly, and perhaps most importantly, you must not share the details of your tests with each other. The tests you will go through are different for every student and the results are for the Curates and Master Pevus to determine your worthiness of bonding with a dragon. If you share your test details, you will immediately be removed from the Citadel and your memory will be magically wiped. You will not remember this place, or of ever being here."

My eyes widened in surprise. I knew less about magic than I did about dragons. The idea that a single person had the power to remove memories was … frightening, at the least. If a sorcerer could do that, what else were they capable of?

"There are other, minor rules, but these three are inarguable. You will not be able to contest them if you are guilty of breaking them. Do you all understand the rules as I have explained them?"

There was more nodding, but Anesko didn't seem satisfied.

"I want to hear your understanding," he said.

"Yes, Curate," a few of us said.

"Everyone at once," he demanded.

"Yes, Curate," all of our voices rose together.

"Excellent. Normally, testing would begin in the morning, but Master Pevus has decided to push it back a day. You are all free tomorrow to enjoy the day as you see fit. I would suggest getting to know your surroundings and learning the maze of hallways. Meals are served at the second bell, the seventh bell, and the thirteenth bell. If you don't eat at the designated times, you don't eat."

This was supposed to be a school. Why were the rules so harsh? Forcing students to go hungry seemed wrong. Granted, going hungry was something I was accustomed to, but still. None of the nobles probably knew what going hungry meant. I found some satisfaction with that idea. A spoiled noble going hungry might teach them something.

"You are all dismissed," Anesko said, then turned on his heel and left.

After he had disappeared from view, Maren loudly joked, "That guy needs to lighten up. Life is not that serious."

I grinned at her, but everyone else ignored her and trekked up the staircase that led to our rooms. Maren and I went up last. She kept glancing around and I had a feeling she was up to something.

"What are you doing tomorrow?" she asked, her voice much lower than before.

"Learning my way around the school," I replied.

"That sounds boring," she huffed. "Want to go see the dragons again? Maybe this time one won't throw up on you and we'll get to touch one."

I stopped mid-step and looked at her incredulously. "Were you not listening to the Curate, or are you itching for trouble? We're not allowed to go into the stables."

"Rules were made to be broken, Eldwin."

"Trust me," I said, raising my mangled hand for her to see. "Rules are in place for good reason."

Maren stared at my hand in silence for a moment, then opened her mouth as if she was going to say something. Instead, she pursed her lips and nodded once, then continued up the stairs. Finally. Maybe she could learn to follow the rules after all.

I stepped into my room, the third door from the

staircase. Simon was already inside. He'd had his belongings delivered by a servant, and his stuff was neatly arranged on one side of the room. I only had the clothes I was wearing. It didn't bother me too much. I tried to look at the bright side. After all, I didn't have to lug around a bunch of things.

I sat on my bed and slipped my worn boots off, then laid back and stared up at the ceiling. From the corner of my eye, I could see that Simon was blatantly ignoring me. I tried to hide my smile, just in case he was looking my way. Maren had a fiery, rebellious personality. That wouldn't be a bad thing if she were a noble, but low borns couldn't get away with acting rash like that.

Still, I found her alluring like a poisonous flower. She was nice to look at, but if you got too close, she would infect you. Perhaps that wouldn't be so bad. So long as she didn't get me kicked out of the Citadel, I could deal with her intrepid nature.

"Hey," Simon said brusquely.

"I know, 'Tell my friend to watch her back.' I got your warning, Simon."

"What are you blabbering on about?" he asked.

I sat up and looked at him. "In the lavatory. I heard your veiled threat about Maren."

Simon looked genuinely confused. "I don't know who you heard, but it wasn't me." He shook his head and muttered something under his breath.

"Right. What did you want to say, then?" I asked.

"I was going to say that I think it would be best if you left now while you have a choice in the matter. That hand isn't going to do you any favors around here."

"How selfless of you," I replied, then laid back down.

"I'm trying to help you keep your honor intact," Simon said. "You may not have been born a noble, but your father's Deed shouldn't be disparaged because you're too stubborn to give up."

"I can't give up," I said. "I have nothing without this school."

There was a long moment of silence. I looked over at Simon to see why he hadn't said anything. He was on his bed, his back to me. I rolled my eyes. How dare he try to tell me what my father's honor was worth? I knew more than anyone, especially some spoiled noble brat. I was still fuming when I heard Simon snoring. It wasn't too loud, but I was having trouble falling asleep and the sound was annoying.

I rolled off the bed and left the room, then headed down the stairs and navigated my way to the lavatory. The stone floor was cold on my feet, but it felt good. I splashed some water from a bucket onto my face and stared into one of the mirrors that hung on the wall.

My eyes were red. I was physically exhausted, but I couldn't sleep. My mind was running in every direction. I headed back to the North Wing intending to try and force myself to sleep, but I saw a shadow dart down the hall to the left. I knew I should have just minded my own business, but my curiosity was piqued, and I slowly followed after the shadow.

As I turned the corner, I recognized Maren. She was surprisingly quiet for how fast she was moving.

"Maren!" I whispered loudly.

She must not have heard me, for she disappeared into the shadows. I almost went after her, but I didn't want to risk being caught by the Curate. I made it back to my room and climbed into bed, then laid there and tried to clear my mind.

When the sun rose and Simon got up, I was still awake. The day was going to be a rough one.

6

I managed to get down to the dining hall in time for breakfast.

There were small mountains of scrambled eggs, buttered toast, and thick sausages piled on the serving table. I wasn't as hungry as I expected to be, so I ate a minimal amount and listened to the conversations around me. A few people talked about how they thought the Curate was rude, and others talked about wanting to see the dragons.

Maren was unsurprisingly absent. I figured she had probably snuck down to see the dragons already. She was going to get caught, I was sure of it. I'd be sad to see her go, but it would be her fault for breaking the rules. I wondered where she had gone last night, but there was no telling. She was a free spirit.

I decided to check out the market in Autumnwick since I doubted that we would get many days to ourselves. I didn't have any money to spend, but I just wanted to get some fresh air. It was surprising that I wasn't falling asleep standing up since I hadn't slept at all the night before.

As I walked down the various aisles of stalls, I saw wares of all kinds. Swords and armor, meats and pastries, and many things I didn't recognize. Since it was still early in the morning, the crowds were light. I stopped at a stall that had daggers and admired the craftsmanship.

One, in particular, caught my eye. The hilt was fashioned in the design of a dragon's head, and the blade was curved like a dragon tooth. It would be a good match for my sword, but I didn't bother asking the vendor how much it cost. Someone came up beside me and I moved aside to give them space.

"Eldwin." It was Simon's voice.

I looked over, surprised to find him in the market. Nobles usually sent servants out for them, but considering he was in the school now, I supposed Simon would have to get used to doing things for himself.

"Simon," I replied tersely.

"I wanted to apologize for what I said last night," he said.

Confusion assaulted my mind. Simon wanted to apologize? I blinked a few times, my mind trying to wrap itself around his words.

"I could have been less abrasive with what I said. It's just hard to hear everyone talking badly about you because of your hand. Your father was a hero, and even though he was low born, it's not right. I was just trying to help."

"Well, you were also talking about my hand."

"I know. I'm sorry."

Simon was confusing me. He was a noble, and nobles were all the same. Selfish, self-absorbed, and high maintenance. Yet here he was apologizing. I would never have imagined a noble apologizing in general, but especially not to me.

"Don't worry about it," I said. "I'm used to it, trust me."

"I want to make it up to you," Simon said.

"You don't have to," I said.

"I want to," he replied. "Come with me."

Simon walked away before I could argue. I watched him and debated on whether or not to follow him. The internal debate lasted a few seconds, then I sighed and hurried to catch up to him. I wasn't too proud.

"Really," I said. "You don't have to do anything."

"It's the least I can do."

Simon turned to the left, away from the market and down an alley. I wasn't sure where he was leading me, but I continued to follow him. Another left took us behind a building. There was a group of guards leaning against the building's wall. A feeling of uneasiness swept over me as I saw the men were city guards.

I started to backstep, but the clink of chainmail alerted me to more guards closing in from behind. I instinctively reached for my sword but remembered it was in the Citadel's armory. My heart started hammering in my chest.

"Well done, Simon," one of the guards said. "I was starting to think he had left the city before I could give him a proper introduction to Autumnwick."

The guard who spoke stepped forward and I recognized him from the other day. He was the one who had accosted Maren before I intervened. I swallowed hard, knowing that whatever he had in store for me, it couldn't be good.

"What's your name?" the guard asked.

I remained silent, but Simon spoke up.

"His name is Eldwin. His father was Matthias Baines."

The guard tilted his head slightly. "The war hero?" he asked.

"The same," Simon answered.

"It's a shame he raised a son who doesn't know how to mind his own business. Either way, I'm going to enjoy teaching him a lesson." He motioned with his hand and the guards behind me grabbed my arms roughly, holding me in place.

"You see, Eldwin, here in Autumnwick, we city guards don't care for dragoons. Granted, you aren't one yet, but you're trying to earn your way in. Do you know why we don't like dragoons?"

I stared back at him, trying to make myself look defiant. If it worked, the guard didn't bother to acknowledge it.

"It's because they let people like you in. Crippled, low born, damaged people. How do they expect people like you to defend the kingdom?" He shook his head. "Look at his blasted hand! He can't even properly hold a sword."

"I can wield a blade," I finally spoke.

"Ah, so now he speaks. I doubt that you have the strength in that hand to hold a real man's sword."

"My father's blade is more of a real man's sword than you've ever seen." Anger was beginning to simmer within me.

"Is that right?" The guard stepped closer, drawing only a few inches from me. I could smell the leather of his armor, along with the scent of his body odor. I scrunched my nose. He needed to take a bath.

"Jon, you said you were only going to scare him a bit," Simon said. I looked at him, but he didn't meet my gaze.

"I am," Jon replied. "But he doesn't seem scared yet."

Pain lanced through my stomach as Jon drove his fist into me. I would have crumbled to my knees if his cronies wouldn't have been holding my arms. I sucked in air between coughs. The realization that Simon had tricked me only made me angrier, but I was outnumbered and overpowered.

"You're pathetic," Jon spat. "You'll always live in your father's shadow. At least he's not alive to see how wretched you are."

Jon punched me again. His guards released my

arms and I fell to the ground. Dust rose and got into my mouth. It made my teeth gritty and I wanted to spit it out, but it was all I could do to breathe.

"Come on, Jon. Just leave him here." It was Simon again. Maybe he felt bad and that was why he was trying to intervene. It didn't matter. He'd betrayed me. Dragoons were supposed to defend the kingdom and protect its people, yet Simon was no better than these petty guards.

"That's a good idea, Simon. I will leave him here. That way, no one will find his body."

I heard ringing steel and looked up to see Jon had drawn his sword. Terror forced my limbs to move, and I struggled to my feet. The guards behind me shoved me back to the ground and my knees struck the dirt painfully.

"What are you doing?" Simon demanded. "You can't murder someone!"

"I can do as I see fit," Jon rebuked.

"I won't let you."

"Watch yourself, Simon. You may be a noble, but my father outranks yours."

I prepared myself to get up and make a run for it as Jon lifted his sword. Simon cried out in protest and grabbed ahold of Jon's arm as Jon started to swing, which threw his motion off. The blade swung narrowly past my face. I crawled backward and bumped into the legs of the guards behind me.

Simon and Jon struggled against one another. I

started to get to my feet, but one of the guards struck me in the head. Agony screamed throughout my body. I gasped and my vision threatened to go black. I fought against unconsciousness, but it was a losing battle.

A bright flash of light and a sound like thunder echoed against the buildings around us. I was already dazed, and the light blinded me, stabbing into my eyes and bursting into the back of my skull like a thousand tiny hot shards of glass.

I screamed, unable to bear the pain, but I couldn't hear myself over the roaring thunder. It seemed like the world was ending, ending in burning light and rumbling noise. I could see faint outlines of the guards rushing past me. Just before the darkness of oblivion took me into its embrace, I thought I saw a face contorted with rage.

Maren's face.

7

When I awoke, I had no idea where I was.

My mind seemed foggy as if it was stuffed with cotton. I was lying on my back, staring up at a white ceiling. I was parched, and my lips were chapped. Running my dry tongue over them was like using sandstone to moisturize.

"Water," I rasped as I tried to sit up.

A wave of nausea washed over me and I had to lie back down. A dull pain throbbed in my stomach, and I vaguely remembered Jon hitting me. It felt like an eternity before the nausea passed and I was able to force myself into a sitting position.

There were two people in the room with me. I immediately recognized Curate Anesko, but I didn't know the other person. It was a woman, and instead of gray or brown robes, she wore white ones. She walked over to me carrying a wooden pitcher and cup. She poured some water into the cup and handed it to me. I started to take a sip but noticed tiny leaves floating in the water. I looked at the woman curiously.

"It'll help with the pain," she said.

I was too thirsty to care whether that was true or not. I drank deeply, downing the entire cup as if I hadn't had water in weeks.

"Where am I?" I choked out as I handed the

empty cup to her. She sprinkled some more leaves into the cup and refilled it.

"The infirmary," she replied. "How are you feeling?"

"Rough," I said. "I've felt worse, though." I held my hand up for emphasis.

"How did I get here?" I asked.

"I'll let Curate Anesko answer that," she said. She glanced back at him and he joined us.

"What were you doing in the market?" Anesko asked. His tone wasn't filled with tenderness like the healer.

"I was browsing the vendors."

"How did you end up behind the money changers building?"

I didn't know what a money changer was, but I assumed he meant the building Simon had led me behind. I opened my mouth to answer and paused. Simon had betrayed me, true, but he also tried to defend me when he realized Jon was going to kill me. I considered whether I owed him any favors, and decided that his actions had canceled each other out. I didn't owe him anything.

"Simon tricked me into going behind the building with a promise of giving me something. The only thing back there was the city guards. They tried to kill me."

Anesko exchanged glances with the healer.

"Drink this," the woman said, then she and

Anesko stepped away and held a whispered conversation.

I couldn't hear what they were saying. A low ringing sound had taken up residence in my ears. I sipped the water and looked around the infirmary. The walls were white like the ceiling, but the floor was the same gray stone as the rest of the Citadel. Rows of beds were lined in orderly rows, all of them empty except one. I hadn't noticed before, but someone was lying in the bed with a bandage wrapped around their torso. A large vibrant red stained the sterile fabric.

Blood. Lots of it.

Anesko and the healer came back over and I turned my attention to them.

"I'm going to escort you to your room," Anesko said. "You can rest there for the remainder of the day. Tomorrow begins the first test, and unfortunately, if you don't test tomorrow, you don't test at all."

"He needs at least three more days to rest," the healer interjected.

"I don't make the rules, Anessa. I enforce them."

"It's fine," I said. "I'm feeling a little rough, but I can take the test."

"Are you sure?" Anessa asked, her face etched with worry.

"I have to. This is my only chance." I couldn't

be sure, but I thought I saw a bit of a smirk on Anesko's lips. Was he proud of me, or was he trying not to laugh at my weakness? I supposed it didn't matter either way.

"If anything happens to him, I will not be pleased," Anessa warned the Curate. Anesko rolled his eyes and offered me his hand. I accepted it and slid off the bed. Without another word, the Curate led me through the infirmary toward the door. As we passed by the bed with the bloodied person, I saw that it was Simon. My eyes widened in surprise.

"What happened to Simon?" I asked.

"He was stabbed," Anesko replied.

"Stabbed?" I remembered his scuffle with Jon. The guard must have gained the upper hand. I clenched my jaw in anger, which only added to my headache. "Will he be all right?"

"Don't worry about him. You have enough of your own problems."

I wasn't sure what Anesko meant by that, and I didn't bother asking. We walked through the hallways in silence. Anesko kept his pace slow enough that I was able to keep up. The pain in my stomach was still there, but it had diminished enough that it was more an annoyance than anything else.

Once we reached the staircase that led up to my floor, Anesko stopped. He turned to face me and I saw that the hardness in his eyes had lessened.

"I don't know why Simon and the city guard have it out for you, but I can only assume it has something to do with who your father is. Perhaps they think that beating on you will gain them some sort of reputation. People are stupid when they are young, and today's events only solidify that for me."

Anesko sighed and rubbed his eyes with the tips of his fingers. He seemed stressed. There had to be more going on than just my situation. I was involved and I wasn't as strained as he was.

"Someone used magic in that fight," he added. "It was a powerful spell, too. I don't think the guards did it. They aren't trained in the ways that students of the Citadel are. Using magic against another person is illegal. I have to ask. Did you use magic against those guards?"

"No," I answered. "I didn't even know that what happened was the result of magic. I was barely conscious when I got blinded."

"Good. Do you know who cast the spell?"

"No, Curate. I didn't see anyone other than the guards. And Simon." The memory of Maren's angry face flashed in my mind's eye. If that was real, I think I did know who cast the spell, but I would never tell anyone.

Anesko frowned. "We will have to find the person who did. Someone with magic that powerful must be trained to properly use it, or they risk the lives of everyone around them."

I nodded, not sure what to say. I just wanted to go back to sleep. I was sure the Curate could see my exhaustion.

"Listen to me, Eldwin. Listen well. The tests are not easy. They will push you in ways you've never dreamed of. It is no small feat to pass the tests, but also know that passing the tests is only scratching the surface of what being a dragoon holds. Did your father ever talk about his time here?"

I shook my head. "No, Curate."

"There is a good reason for that, trust me. Before the testing is done, you will wish that you were dead. I know I did."

"Thank you for letting me know," I said.

Anesko stared at me, his eyes probing my soul, looking for any hesitation or weakness. I was determined to pass the tests. Being a dragoon was all there was for me. If I didn't pass and bond with a dragon, I had no idea what I would do, or where I would go. The lands my father's Deed had earned were dead like my parents. No crops grew there and water was non-existent. This was all I had.

The Curate placed a hand on my shoulder. "Get some rest," he said. "You're going to need it."

And then he left. I stood there for a moment, running his words through my mind, over and over. I made my way up the stairs slowly. Every muscle in my body was sore. By the time I reached the top, I was tempted to get on my knees and crawl the rest of the way. Yet somehow, I had enough strength to make it to my room and into bed. I fell asleep almost immediately.

I awoke to the sound of the Citadel's bell ringing and quickly sat up. What bell was it? What *day* was it? I rolled out of bed and was happy to find that other than a dull soreness in my stomach, I felt completely rested. At the foot of my bed was a folded set of gray robes. I figured I was supposed to wear them, so I put them on over my clothes and headed down to the dining hall. It was empty aside from a few servants doing some cleaning.

"What bell is it?" I asked one of them.

"Fifth," the man answered.

I thanked him and then sprinted for the temple, hoping I wasn't too late.

8

I rushed into the temple.

To my relief, everyone was seated and appeared to be waiting for Master Pevus. I slipped into the last pew, trying to be as quiet as possible. Nobody appeared to notice my tardiness, or if they did, they didn't care.

I spotted Maren sitting in one of the middle rows. I thought about how I had seen her face during my attack. There had been so much rage in her eyes. Thinking about it now gave me a chill. Was she the one who had cast the powerful spell Curate Anesko mentioned? I didn't know.

Wait.

I considered the many odd statements she'd said. Things about people wanting to help her for personal gain. What if she was a sorcerer? That thought gave me pause. The only sorcerer I had ever met was an old hedge witch when I was eight. I'd been violently ill and my mother had tried every remedy she could think of, but nothing worked.

In desperation, she'd taken me to see Yizell. The old witch had looked ancient and moved slow, but she was kind and offered a concoction that ended my sickness. Given that it was my only interaction with a magic user, it was hard to fathom the anger one of them could possess. And yet, if it was Maren who had cast the spell … she had done it to save me.

Master Pevus strode into the room then, his robes fluttering around him. He stood on the raised dais and cleared his throat. I squinted at him. He looked like he had aged several years since I had seen him the other night.

"Attention! Attention, students!"

Once the multitude of voices quieted, Master Pevus continued.

"Today we will begin Compassion, the first of three tests. Only one student will be tested at a time. As such, we will break for meals. Given that this is such a large group, I'm hoping that we will be finished before the curfew bell, but I am not completely in control of the test.

"The magic of the temple is the true master here, and it will dictate the amount of time you will spend in the test. I believe the longest any potential student has spent been in the test was three hours, but that is certainly not the norm."

Master Pevus motioned at a door to his right.

"This door will lead you into the chamber where you will be tested. The Curates and I will view the testing, but we will not interfere unless it is deemed an emergency."

Someone in the front raised their hand.

"Yes?"

"Is the test dangerous?" the person asked.

"Physically, no. At least, not that I've ever

witnessed. Mentally, however, is another matter." Master Pevus paused as if he was uncertain about how to elaborate. "These tests are designed to investigate the deepest parts of you, the ones that you may not even be aware of. Sometimes the tested can be temporarily … damaged, for lack of a better term. But there are no lasting effects."

"What happens if you fail the first test?" someone else asked.

Master Pevus steepled his fingers and stared down at them for a moment, then looked back up.

"If you fail the first test, your memories of this place and what you did here will be magically erased. This is for your safety, as well as ours. If you pass the Compassion test, then you will move on to Magical Aptitude."

One of the Curates, I didn't know her name, walked up to Master Pevus and whispered something to him. He nodded and smiled broadly.

"We are ready to begin the testing. We will start at the first pew and work our way back. Out of respect for your fellows, I ask that you keep the noise to a minimum."

Master Pevus pointed to the person sitting at the edge of the first pew.

"Will you please join me up here?"

I recognized the person from my first day. He'd been in the group that I had walked in with when we were assigned rooms with the Provost. I didn't know his name, but he was a low born with brown hair. Master Pevus led him to the door, where one of the Curates opened it. The master ushered him inside, then the Curate closed the door.

Both the master and the Curate left the room through another door and the rest of us sat in silence. I was hoping there would be some sort of sound or something that let us know the test had started, but I was disappointed when nothing happened. Eventually, people started having whispered conversations.

After a quarter of an hour, Master Pevus came back into the room and called up the next person. And so it went, over and over, until the seventh bell. We were released for lunch, and then we went back to the temple. The process continued. I wondered where the tested exited the chamber, for they didn't come out of the door they entered in. I'd find out myself soon enough.

When we came back from lunch, everyone had moved to the front rows and changed spots. I stayed near the back. I wasn't scared to take the test, but I wasn't jumping in excitement, either. This was the first step towards proving I was worthy of being a dragoon, and I wasn't sure if I was ready.

Maren sat next to me. I looked at her and she smiled. She didn't seem any different. Perhaps I had imagined her face?

"Are you nervous?" she asked.

"A little, I guess. What about you?"

"Nope. Why are you nervous?"

I shrugged. "I guess because if I fail, I have nowhere to go."

"What about your family's land? And your mother?"

"My mother died," I said softly. "A few weeks before I left to come here. She had the wasting sickness."

Maren frowned and laid her left hand atop my right. My mangled one.

"I'm sorry," she said.

I could feel my eyes well with tears, but I refused to cry. I blinked rapidly.

"What about the land? You get to keep it by birthright."

"I know, but the land is dead. Crops won't grow, and all of the people who worked for my family left after my father died in battle. I am a noble in name only. There is no money, no food, nothing. The Citadel is *all* I have."

Maren squeezed my hand and in some unexplainable way, I felt comforted. We didn't talk much after that. And even though we were just waiting, the time went by quickly. When our pew was the last, I began to get anxious. My palms got sweaty and my heart started beating faster. Maren didn't let go of my hand until it was her turn to enter the chamber.

"See you on the other side," she said, grinning.

I watched her until she disappeared into the

chamber, then I leaned forward and looked down at the floor. I was next after her, and there were two people after me. I considered asking them to switch places with me, but there was no reason to delay the inevitable. I had spent so much time looking forward to this moment, and now that it was here, I could hardly believe it. I was following in my father's footsteps.

I closed my eyes and inhaled deep, measured breaths. My mind needed to be clear so I could focus. I pushed everything from my mind and thought only about the dragon from the stables. It had been too dark to see what color it was, but I remembered its glowing eyes and its razor-sharp teeth. To bond with a creature like that, to share in its strengths and weaknesses, was hard to imagine, but I knew it was what I wanted.

By the time Master Pevus entered the room and called me to the front, I had calmed my nerves and was ready for the test. He had called it Compassion. While I didn't know what the test would be like, I knew what compassion was. My mother had been the only person who didn't look at me differently after my hand had been crushed. She'd shown me compassion every day.

I walked to the front and followed the master to the door. Curate Anesko opened the door and I glanced back at Master Pevus one last time. His forehead was stooped with worry, but he'd looked like that all day, so I didn't let it bother me. His eyes were a faded blue, almost gray. He smiled at me, and I felt assurance in his expression. I nodded at him, then looked at Anesko as I walked through the doorway.

The Curate offered a single nod. I bowed my head to him, then looked ahead. The chamber looked like every other room of the Citadel with its smooth stone walls and floor. But when the door closed behind me, everything changed.

9

I was in Autumnwick's market.

The Citadel towered behind me and I wondered if the magic of the test had actually transported me here. Everything was strikingly real, so it must have. It made sense, considering I hadn't seen anyone come out of the testing chamber. I wasn't sure what I was supposed to do, so I began to explore the market.

A young boy was standing beside one of the vendor stalls, watching as people passed by. He was a low born with black hair and couldn't be older than eight years. His face was dirty, and his clothes were in serious disrepair. As I walked by, he called out to me.

"Mister! Do you have any coins to spare?"

Instinctively, I reached for my coin purse before remembering that I had no money. I patted the purse anyway, and I shook my head at the boy.

"Sorry, I don't."

The boy's eyes gazed at me as if he was able to discern whether I was being truthful or not. He tilted his head to the side and smiled. A few of his teeth were missing.

"That's all right. May your luck improve!"

"Yours, too," I replied.

I continued walking through the market and went down a row I hadn't seen the other day. There were two people at a stall about mid-way down the aisle. They were having a heated discussion, and one of them was waving their arms about wildly. I thought about going down another row, but curiosity got the better of me and I slowly got closer to them.

"I saw it first," a woman said.

"Maybe, but I asked to buy it first," the other woman retorted.

I glanced at the vendor, and he seemed content to let the women verbally duel it out between themselves.

"It's the last one, and I need it."

I peered between the women and saw that they were arguing over a slaughtered pig. The amount of meat it would provide should have been adequate for two families. I held my tongue as I listened to their exchange, but then one of the women started to act like she was going to resort to violence.

"You going to say something?" I asked the vendor. He glanced at me for a moment, then looked away and ignored me.

"Ladies," I interrupted.

At first, they didn't acknowledge me. They kept yelling at one another and even started hurling insults. If someone didn't do something quickly, I was certain the two would end up hitting each other.

"Ladies," I repeated, louder this time. That got their attention.

"What do you want, boy?" It was the one who said she asked to buy the pig first.

"Isn't that more than enough meat for one family?"

The woman looked at the pig, then back at me. "And?"

"Could you two not split the cost, then half the meat so that both of you get to enjoy it?" It seemed like common sense to me, but the look on the woman's face revealed that she hadn't even considered the idea.

"I … I suppose," she said, her anger quickly deflating. She looked back at the other woman and seemed embarrassed. "That does sound like a good idea to me. What about you?"

"Yes, I like that idea, too."

The first woman turned to the vendor and asked him to cut the meat and divide it evenly. The vendor seemed disappointed that the situation had been diffused, but he obliged her request anyway.

Satisfied that I had helped, I was about to continue walking down the row when the first woman laid a hand on my shoulder. I turned around and she held out a silver coin to me.

"Please, take this," she said. "As a sign of my appreciation."

"I can't accept that," I said.

The woman pressed the coin into my palm, ignoring my weak protest. I tightened my grip on the coin and the woman offered me a smile and a single nod, then turned back to watch the vendor cut the pig in half.

I held the coin up. It flashed in the sunlight and appeared to be newly minted. The inscriptions on the coin's surface weren't familiar to me. In fact, I was certain that the coin wasn't even from our kingdom. That didn't mean it lacked value, so I put it into my coin purse and continued down the rest of the row.

There was nothing that caught my interest, so I headed back to the front of the market where I had started. I decided this wasn't much of a test, especially since I didn't know what I should be doing. The boy begging for coins was still in the same spot. He looked at me and waved. And then an idea came to me.

Compassion.

What if I was meant to get the coin from the woman, only to give it to the child? I walked over to the boy and knelt in front of him, then dug the coin from my purse and held it out to him.

"Here," I said. "You need this more than I do."

The boy smirked, his eyes glittering with mischievousness.

"I see your luck turned around quickly!" he said.

"So it did."

"I don't need your coin," the boy said.

"Oh. Well, I figured since you asked me earlier …"

The boy was shaking his head before I could finish speaking. He pushed my hand away gently just as a tremor shook the ground. The vibrations made my knees shake and I glanced around the market to see if anyone else had noticed the disturbance.

It was business as usual. When I looked at the boy again, his facial expression had darkened. He stepped closer to me and whispered harshly, "He's coming!"

"Who is?" I asked.

The boy grew fearful and he looked back and forth frantically. It made me uneasy and I too looked around. I didn't see anything out of the ordinary. People were making purchases and having conversations like normal, so I was confused by the boy's fear.

"Who is coming?" I repeated.

The boy's small hands gripped my shirt and he stared into my eyes.

"The False King is coming," he whispered harshly.

"Who is that?"

Dark clouds began to appear in the sky and thunder rumbled in the distance. The storm was brewing quickly, much more quickly than seemed normal. Within moments, the sun was blotted out and lightning flickered among the clouds.

Odder still, the boy's eyes were glowing with a dull blue light. I fell backward and scrambled away on my hands and feet. The boy turned to the storm clouds and raised his hands. Flames flickered to life on his fingertips, casting dancing shadows around him.

The storm clouds grew thicker and darker, sucking all light into their black void. The people that had been in the market were gone. I realized that the buildings and tents were also gone. The market had simply vanished. It was only the boy and myself.

And the figure in the storm.

A lone form detached from the darkness and strode purposefully toward the boy. The flames on the boy's fingers arced high and formed a fiery pattern in the air, keeping the figure from getting any closer.

Even in the growing darkness, the boy's magic glowed brightly, defending us from the shadows. The figure struggled to get past the magical shield, but it was too strong. I had no idea what was happening. Was this part of the test? What did any of this have to do with compassion?

"I demand you leave!" the boy shouted at the figure. "You are not welcome here!"

"You can't stop me forever," the figure finally spoke. His voice made my flesh crawl. It was as if spiders were swarming along my skin. A wave of panic spread throughout me when I saw the magical barrier shudder and give way before the darkness.

The boy screamed, and there was nothing but the darkness.

I closed my eyes, preparing for my inevitable death. And then I heard a familiar voice.

"Eldwin."

I looked up to see Master Pevus and Curate Anesko standing in a doorway that blended with the stone wall of the testing chamber.

"Is it over?" I asked. "Is the test done?"

"It's done," Master Pevus said. "Come."

It was finally over. The strange boy, the magic, the dark figure that had snuffed out the light. My heart still pounded heavily in my chest. The cold stones of the floor were comforting and I stayed where I was for a long moment, then rose to my feet. It had all seemed so real and I had thought for sure that I was really in the market, but no. I was in the chamber the entire time. That brought some relief to my anxiousness. It was all just part of the test.

Curate Anesko was leading us through a hallway that curved like a crescent.

"Master?" I said.

"Yes?"

"In the test, there was a—"

"Silence!" Master Pevus shouted. "I told you all that what happens in the test is for the tested."

"Yes, but—"

"No," he interrupted again, his tone softer this time. "What you saw was only for you."

I didn't bother trying to ask again. For the rest of the walk, I replayed the test in my mind, over and over. There was so much that didn't make any sense to me, but perhaps it wasn't supposed to. Curate Anesko opened a door at the end of the hall on the left and he motioned me inside. I went in and saw all of the students who had already been tested. I saw Maren and made my way to where she was sitting.

"That was wild, wasn't it?" she said.

I nodded.

"You all right?"

"Yeah," I answered softly, still burdened with my thoughts. I remembered the coin and reached into my purse. Cold metal touched my hand and I grabbed ahold of it and drew it out.

The coin was real.

10

"Gods," I breathed.

"What?" Maren asked. "What is that?"

"It's from my te—" I caught myself and glanced around the room to make sure no one had heard me. I lowered my voice and leaned closer to her.

"It's from my test," I said. "A woman gave it to me. The test isn't real, so how did this coin come back with me?"

"Now who's breaking the rules?" Maren regarded me with a smirk, but seeing my seriousness, she went quiet and placed her hand next to my ear and whispered, "What do you know about magic?"

"Almost nothing," I replied.

"Meet me tonight after curfew and I'll share some things with you."

I would have argued with her about following the rules. Now, I was too curious to object. I nodded at her, then turned my attention to the front of the room as Master Pevus and the Curates entered. The multitude of conversations died abruptly.

"Thank you," the master said. "Due to unforeseen circumstances, the last few potentials will not be able to take their test in the chamber. For us to keep in line with the rules, they will be tested by the Curates in a series of exercises we employed in the past before the chamber was built."

Master Pevus paused briefly and I wondered if what happened in my test had anything to do with the sudden turn of events.

"Those of you who have already taken the assessment may go to dinner. Remember that you are not to discuss the details of your trials with the other potentials. Unless you have any questions for myself or the Curates, you are dismissed."

Everyone stood and began to file out of the room. Maren and I followed the others out of the chamber and made our way to the dining hall. The conversations were muted, and everyone seemed tired or distracted. The master hadn't been kidding when he said the test would push you in ways you didn't think were possible.

I barely ate anything at all and ended up pushing the food around on my plate more times than I could count. The curfew bell was still a few hours away, so I took advantage of the time and went to the infirmary to check on Simon. With the chaos of the day, I hadn't devoted much time to thinking about him and I was feeling guilty.

The healer who had helped me was there changing Simon's bandages when I arrived. She glanced at me as I entered, but she didn't say anything. Once she was finished, she carried the dirty bandages away and I stood beside Simon's bed. The clean wrappings were already stained with blood. I frowned and looked at Simon's face. His eyes were closed, but they fluttered slightly.

"I don't know if you can hear me," I said softly, "but I want to thank you for saving my life. I know you were the cause of me getting into that situation anyway, but you could have left me for dead. I know I wasn't born into nobility like you, but I think all life is valuable, regardless of your social status. I'm hoping you pull through this injury and …" And what? I felt like I was beginning to ramble.

"And, uh, maybe once you are healed, we might end up as friends or something. Thank you again, Simon."

I turned and left the infirmary, then headed back to my room to get some rest. Considering I hadn't slept the night before and the day had been full of stress, I was surprised I hadn't passed out from sheer exhaustion yet. I pulled my boots off and collapsed into bed. The next thing I knew, Maren was gently shaking my shoulder.

"Wake up," she whispered.

Judging by the lack of light in the room, I figured it was late. I sat up and rubbed the sleep from my eyes.

"Sorry," I mumbled. "I was supposed to meet you."

"Don't worry about it," Maren replied. "We can talk here since your roommate is in the infirmary."

"Sure," I said. I cleared my throat and pushed myself back against the headboard.

"Can I see that coin again?"

I fished it out of my coin purse and handed it to her. Maren held it close to her face for a long moment, then nodded and handed it back.

"You told me you don't know much about magic," she said. "Sorcerers are secretive in nature, so most people don't know anything about what they do."

I was fully awake now, and my earlier suspicions about Maren hiding something were at the forefront of my mind. Before I could stop myself, I blurted out, "You're hiding something."

"What do you mean?" she asked. Her facial expression was flawless, but the tone in her voice let me know that I wasn't wrong.

"You're hiding something," I repeated. "I think I know what it is. You don't have to worry; I'm not going to share your secret."

She stared at me in silence and chewed her lower lip nervously. "Yes, I have a secret," she said. "I'm—"

"A sorcerer?" I interrupted. "I figured. You were there in the alley when Jon and his guards attacked me, weren't you?"

Maren heaved a sigh and seemed relieved. "Yes, I was there."

"Curate Anesko said they are looking for whoever cast that spell. He said it was powerful."

"It wasn't my best work," she admitted. "I don't know what came over me. I saw you in danger and just … acted. I'm sorry I almost killed you."

I swallowed hard and tried to act like it wasn't a big deal, but I had just gained a healthy fear of her. "Thank you for what you did." I held the coin up. "Now tell me about this. How did it come with me out of the test?"

"I'll try to," Maren replied. "Magic is like the wind. You can't see it, but you can feel it. You know when it's there. And like the wind, it chooses its own path. Why did the magic of the chamber give you that coin? I don't know. That doesn't mean there isn't a purpose, though. Even though most people don't know much about magic, it is inside all of us. Not everyone can use it, but for some people, it just needs to be awakened."

"How do I find out what the purpose of the coin is?" I asked, still trying to understand her explanation.

"You'll have to figure that out for yourself. Like the master said about the tests, it is different for everyone. Speaking of, how was your test? You said a woman gave you that coin?"

I glanced at the open door, suddenly afraid that someone might be listening to our conversation. Maren followed my gaze, then looked back at me.

"Did you hear something?" she asked.

"No," I replied. "I guess I'm just nervous. My test seemed fairly normal at first, but then it got weird."

"Weird?" Maren's eyebrow rose. "What do you

mean?"

"A storm came and a figure made of shadows stepped out of the clouds. He got into a magical battle with a small boy."

"That *is* weird," Maren said. "Do you remember anything else?"

"Yeah. The boy was young, and he seemed afraid of something. He said someone was coming."

"Who?"

I tried to remember what the boy said. Was it something about a king? I wracked my brain. "I can't remember exactly. Some king, I think."

"A king is coming?" Maren asked. "But we have a king. That doesn't make any sense."

"Tell me about it. Nothing the boy said seemed to make any sense to me. He was afraid of whoever it was, though. And then he tried to keep the figure away with a spell that created a wall or something."

"This sounds vaguely familiar," Maren said.

"It does?"

"Yes." She nodded. "I heard something about it in my history books."

I closed my eyes and tried to remember the sequence of events in the test. *The woman gave me the coin. I tried to give it to the boy. The storm came. The boy said 'he's coming.'* My eyes snapped open.

"I remember now. He said 'the False King is

coming.'"

The look on Maren's face made the hairs on my arms raise. It was almost as if she was seeing a ghost behind me. I ran my hands down my arms, pushing the hair down and trying to ignore the odd feeling of dread in my stomach.

"What?"

"Don't you know who the False King is?" Maren asked.

"I don't think so?"

"How do you not know, Eldwin? The battle your father died in was against the False King."

I'd honestly never heard the name before, but suddenly knowing that he was the cause of my father's death made me hate him, and I didn't even know who he was.

"Who's the False King?" I asked.

11

Maren stared at me in disbelief.

"You really don't know the story?" She sighed and shook her head. "It's a long tale, but I'm not going to tell it to you. Do you know how to read?"

"Yes," I said.

"Good. You should go to the library and find the books about him and find out for yourself who he is."

Obviously, I'd rather she just tell me, but considering I had already learned how stubborn she could be, I conceded.

"That's a good idea," I said.

"Those are the only kind I have," Maren said with a smirk.

I rolled my eyes. "You looked worried when I mentioned that king," I said.

"Once you learn about him, you'll understand why. If the chamber was warning you about his return, I think you should tell the master."

"I tried to," I said. "He wouldn't let me say anything about my test, though."

Maren frowned. "Something is going on, but I'm not sure what it could be. Didn't Master Pevus seem stressed all day?"

"Yeah," I answered. "But I think it's because he was dealing with the testing."

"Possibly, but we need to find out for sure."

"We? *We* don't need to do anything, Maren. You've got to stop breaking the rules or you'll be kicked out of the school."

She continued talking as if I hadn't said anything. "Master Pevus and the Curates hold a daily meeting early in the morning, before the first bell. I know a spot where we'll be hidden but can hear everything."

"Maren, I told you—"

"Yes, yes. You don't want to be kicked out, I got it. I'll just go by myself, then."

I knew I couldn't let her do that, but I was afraid of getting caught. And I certainly wouldn't want anyone reporting her to Curate Anesko. I heaved a sigh. "Where is this hidden spot?"

A few hours later, before the sun had yet to rise, Maren and I stood before a stone wall beside the school's council chamber. She was slowly feeling along the stones, but I wasn't sure why. As I was about to open my mouth to issue a complaint, she stood up straight and said, "There!"

There was a grating noise, then a section of the wall pulled back and slid to the side. There was a small room, roughly large enough to hold about five or six people. Maren ushered me inside and the wall glided back into place behind us.

"What is this place?" I asked.

Maren clamped a hand over my mouth. "Ssh! You have to be quiet in here or they'll hear you," she furiously whispered.

"Sorry," I mouthed.

"They're already talking," she said. Maren knelt and motioned me to do the same. I obeyed and sat on the floor beside her. She pointed at the wall and leaned closer to it. I didn't know what she was doing, but I mimicked her. To my surprise, I was able to see through part of the wall and into the council room.

"I saw it as well," Curate Anesko said.

"We all saw it," Master Pevus replied. He looked more haggard than he had earlier if that were possible.

"Yes, but what does it mean?" another Curate asked. I was fairly certain her name was Josephine.

"I'm not sure," the master said. "The magic was warning us, but I don't see how the False King could still be alive. He and Matthias fell in battle. I was there."

"They're talking about your test," Maren murmured. I thought so, too.

"Perhaps sending a scout or two to check things out would do well to ease our fears?" Anesko suggested.

"That's a good idea," Master Pevus said. "Send two dragoons who ride blues. Their speed will get them there and back within a few days."

"Let's hope that we're just seeing monsters in the dark that aren't truly there," Josephine said.

"Yes, let us hope so."

There was silence for a moment, then Master Pevus changed the subject. "What of the manual testing? How did that go?"

"Very well, considering we've not done it in my lifetime," Anesko replied. "They both passed, according to the documents."

"That is good news. Based on the chamber tests, are we all in agreement on those who passed and those who failed?"

The Curates all spoke at once, but the consensus seemed to be agreement. I wondered who had failed. Was I one of them? My stomach churned with anxiety.

"There is one final matter to discuss before we dismiss." The master leaned back in his chair and rubbed his eyes while stifling a yawn. "The girl."

The room went quiet. I glanced at Maren, but she kept her eyes on Master Pevus.

"Her identity is unknown to the others," Anesko said. "I've listened to the conversations all day. No one is talking about her."

"It's bound to come out sooner or later," the master said. "I'm not worried about that, but I am concerned about her safety. If something happens to her …" he let the words hang in the air. The Curates glanced at one another, but no one spoke.

"She knew the risks in coming here," Anesko said. "The power she has doesn't change that. And it doesn't change how she is tested, either."

"I agree," Master Pevus said. "Her father is the one that poses the most problematic if something goes wrong. From the reports I've received, he doesn't even know she's gone."

"Then we feign ignorance if he finds out she's missing and that she's here," Anesko said. "Politics have no place here."

The master laughed. "You still have much to learn if you believe that."

Anesko folded his arms. "Our task is to train dragon riders. So long as we are doing that, I don't see what her father would take issue with."

"I don't disagree with that," Master Pevus replied. "Regardless, we all need to agree with her presence here."

"I see nothing wrong with it," Josephine said.

"Neither do I," Anesko added.

The other Curates agreed and Master Pevus stood up.

"It's decided, then. She stays and will take the tests like any other potential. If her father becomes a problem, I will deal with him."

That last part didn't sound threatening, but more a statement of fact. I wasn't sure who they were talking about. My first thought was Maren, but the only thing different about her than everyone else was that she was a sorcerer. Maybe her father was also a sorcerer, a powerful one, and they feared his anger if he found out she was here without permission?

"The council is dismissed," Master Pevus said.

Maren and I waited until the room was empty and we didn't hear anyone in the hallway before exiting the hidden chamber.

"Who do you think they were talking about?" I asked.

"We didn't learn anything we didn't already know," Maren huffed in disappointment. "Maybe their scouts will bring back some news that confirms the return of the False King."

"Based on what I've heard so far, I hope he's not back."

"That's something I think everyone would agree with," Maren replied.

We parted ways at the end of the hall, and I headed back to my room. It was still early, and the first bell hadn't rung yet, so I didn't pass anyone else on my way. There was so much going on already and I had only been at the school for a few days. It seemed that more mysteries developed by the moment, and there were more questions than answers.

I made it to my room and paced back and forth, replaying the council meeting over in my mind. The magic of the testing chamber had spoken to me, that was clear. And it had given me the coin. I retrieved it and held it up, staring at its engraving. Maren had said that magic was like the wind and none knew its course, so how was I supposed to know what the coin was for?

"What is your secret?" I whispered. The coin remained silent, as I expected. If it had replied, I would likely have woken the entire school by screaming. I put the coin back in my purse and put on my robes. I yawned and considered how messed up my sleeping schedule had become. Hopefully, it would get back to normal soon.

I needed to find some time to get to the library and read about the False King. Maren had given me almost no information, and my curiosity was rising like a wave. As impatient as I was, the time passed quickly and the first bell clanged, signaling it was time to wake up. I joined my fellow students at the bottom of the stairway, and we found Curate Anesko waiting for us.

"Good morning," he greeted.

"Good morning, Curate," we sounded off.

"This year's potentials are having an easy beginning. The master has declared today a free day, but do not get lax. Tomorrow the testing resumes, and it will be an interesting time. Remember the rules you agreed to and stay away from the dragon stables."

The Curate left and the other potentials scattered throughout the Citadel. It was time to find out who the False King was.

12

The library was located at the far north end of the Citadel. Maren had given me directions during breakfast and I only got turned around twice before reaching the wooden doors that marked the entrance.

I stepped inside and was surprised to find that the place was immaculate. Hundreds, if not thousands, of bookstands were lined in orderly rows. There were several tables and chairs near the windows, where natural light slanted in through the glass panes. A few students were sitting at some of the tables, large tomes opened in front of them. The most notable thing about the library was the silence.

A robed woman sat behind a large desk. She was slowly flipping pages of a book as I walked up. She paused and looked up at me. I remembered her from my first day.

"Surrel," I said, smiling at her.

"Son of Matthias," she replied. "How are you finding the school so far?"

"It's different from what I'm used to, but in a good way."

"That's good to hear. I've been a student for almost a year and I can't say I've had a bad experience yet. How about your testing?"

"I'm not sure," I admitted. "I think I did well

with Compassion, but we haven't heard our results yet."

"No news is good news, as they say," Surrel said. "Normally, the tests are done over three straight days. I've heard there have been some complications, and the testing has been pushed back?"

I nodded. "Yes, our next test will be tomorrow."

"Well, I wish you luck. Have you been to the library yet?"

"No," I said.

"I think you'll like it. We've got the largest collection of books in the entire kingdom," Surrel said proudly. "If you are looking for books on a specific topic, you can search the index for book locations. Here, let me show you."

Surrel stood and walked around the desk. I followed her to a cabinet with hundreds of small drawers. Each drawer was labeled with a metal plaque inscribed with letters.

"Everything is arranged in alphabetical order. So, if you are looking for a book on felines, you will open the drawer that has 'FE' on it. Then you'll flip through the parchments until you find the word you are looking for. Don't remove it from the order it's in. If you do, the Librarian will have a fit."

To show what she meant, Surrel found the parchment labeled feline and lifted it, but not completely out of the drawer.

"Listed on the parchment will be the locations of any book that covers the topic." She pointed to the writing. "R Six-C Three-S Two is the location of a book."

"Am I supposed to memorize that since I can't take the parchment out?"

Surrel giggled. "No, of course not. We have blank parchments, quills, and ink wells available for use. You'll just write down the locations, then take your parchment with you to find the books."

"I can take books from the shelf?" I asked.

"Yes, so long as they are not chained to the shelf. If they are chained, you'll have to read the book there. Chained books are too valuable to be removed."

"Do I have to put the books back when I'm done?"

"We prefer that you didn't," Surrel said. "Just leave the books on the table when you are done and we will ensure they get put back in their proper place." Surrel looked past me to a student who was standing at her desk. "Feel free to start looking through the library. If you need anything, you can find me at the desk there unless I'm helping someone find something."

"Thank you, Surrel. You've been very helpful."

She smiled and walked away. I looked at the vast number of drawers and was glad that my mother had taught me to read and write when I was younger. I found the drawer marked with FA and flipped through the parchments until I found what I was looking for. False King. I retrieved a blank parchment and dipped a quill into an ink well, then took them back to the cabinet and wrote down the first three locations of books.

I closed the drawer and walked along the shelves, completely confused. I had no idea what the locations meant, and there were no obvious markings on the bookstands. After several frustrating moments, I gave up and went to get help from Surrel. She was sitting at her desk scribbling notes. She looked up as I approached.

"I'm sorry for interrupting you," I said, "but I can't seem to figure out how to find these locations."

"Oh! I apologize!" She said loudly, then quickly lowered her voice in embarrassment. "I forgot to explain the locations. Let me see your parchment."

I handed it to her and she pointed to the first one. "The first set of letters and numbers is the row number. You can find the row numbers at the top of the bookstand, on the upper left-hand corner. So, 'R sixteen' stands for Row Sixteen. The second set is the case number, which is the section. So 'C twelve' stands for Case Twelve. And the final number is the shelf position on that case."

"Now that you've explained it, it makes sense. I don't know how I didn't figure that out on my own."

"Don't worry about it," Surrel said. "Most of us never figured it out on our own."

"Thank you again," I said.

Armed with new information, I easily found the first location. The shelf contained about fifty books, but none of them were about the False King. Assuming someone already had that book, I went to the second location on my parchment but found the same problem. The third location was also lacking the book I needed.

I scratched my chin and headed back to the cabinet to find more locations. I wrote down three more, then searched those locations. Again, each shelf was lacking anything about the False King. Growing frustrated, I went back to Surrel's desk. She was absent, so I waited for her to come back. A short moment later, she returned.

"I'm not sure if I'm looking incorrectly, but I don't see the books I'm looking for in these locations." I held out the parchment to Surrel.

She took it and looked at, then motioned for me to follow her. I was worried I had searched erroneously and she was going to make me look like a fool. However, she went to the same location I had and perused the books on the shelf.

"Someone may have this book," she said softly.

"That's what I thought," I replied. "Yet I looked for six different books and none of them are here."

"That is a little odd, though someone may be researching the topic. Let's check a few of the other locations."

Surrel and I went back to the cabinet, and she

wrote down a few more locations. Her handwriting was much smoother than mine. She led the way to the various locations, and each time we encountered the same thing. She seemed to be growing frustrated.

"Let's go to the chained books," she suggested.

The rows of bookstands with chained books took up much less space in the library than the regular books. We went to the location and Surrel frowned.

"Now this *is* odd," she muttered. She pushed a few of the books apart. Hidden behind the books was a piece of a broken chain. A gasp escaped Surrel and she looked at me, her eyes wide.

"This is bad," she whispered. "Very bad. The Librarian is going to be furious that someone took a chained book."

I was less concerned about that than she was and more concerned that every book on the False King was inexplicably missing from the library. Surrel left me to find the Librarian, and I checked a few other locations with no luck. Giving up, I left the library and wandered around the Citadel, letting my thoughts drift. Maren knew about the False King, so I started looking for her. I had a feeling she was down in the dragon stables, and I wasn't going down there.

The seventh bell rang and I went to the dining hall for lunch. Maren was there eating at a table by herself. I filled a tray of food and joined her.

"You'll never believe what happened in the library," I said.

"What?" Maren asked with a mouth full of partially chewed food.

"All of the books on the False King are missing. Even the chained books."

Maren stopped chewing and stared at me. "Are you serious?"

"Yes. Surrel even looked with me. She said the Librarian is going to be upset that someone broke the chains."

"Eldwin," Maren whispered. "Someone stole those books, I'm sure of it."

"That's what I figured," I replied.

"There's only one reason someone would take them."

"Why is that?" I asked.

"Someone is trying to hide something."

13

"Who would be trying to hide something related to the False King?" I asked.

"One of his servants, obviously," Maren replied. "There must be a servant here in the Citadel. A spy relaying information back to the False King."

"We don't even know if the False King is back," I pointed out.

"Always assume your enemy is two steps ahead of you."

I was familiar with the saying. My father said it a lot when I was younger. I never understood it back then, but I did now.

Maren lowered her voice. "I bet it's one of the Curates."

"Why would you think that?" I asked.

"Well, it could be Master Pevus, but I don't think he'd be so stressed if he were the False King's agent. So that leaves the Curates. Think about it. They have access to almost everything in the Citadel, and they are in the council meetings. That makes them privy to a lot of information."

I didn't want to admit it, but she had a point. "Let the master know what you think and see what he says."

Maren was shaking her head before I finished

speaking. "No. I'll need more than just my theory to sway Master Pevus into believing that one of his trusted people is a spy. I'll need proof."

I knew where she was going and sighed.

"We need to follow the Curates around and see what we can find."

"You do know that none of this is your responsibility, right? It's not your job to find a spy if there even is one."

Maren stated at me in silence and judging by the look on her face, it seemed I had hurt her feelings somehow. The look quickly disappeared and was replaced by her customary stubbornness.

"If you don't want to help find who is trying to help the False King, that's fine. I can do it alone." She stood up and left the table, leaving her tray of food mostly uneaten. I shoved a roll into my mouth and hurried after her, chewing furiously.

"I do want to help," I said. "I'm just not sure how well this will go if we get caught by the spy."

"What do you mean?" Maren asked.

"Well, I would assume that if the False King put a spy here, they would powerful."

"Of course."

"And we're barely initiates," I added.

"Did you forget that I'm a sorcerer?"

"No," I said. "But have you ever fought another sorcerer?"

Maren's silence gave me the answer I needed.

"I'm not planning on confronting them myself," she said. "I just need proof that I can take to Master Pevus."

This plan didn't seem very thought out, but for some inexplicable reason, I continued to follow Maren toward trouble.

It turned out that there were many hidden rooms like the one we'd hidden in when we listened to the council meeting. The fact that Maren had memorized their locations after seeing a map of the school was beyond impressive. Maybe sorcerers were gifted with better minds than those of us who weren't magically inclined?

We snuck into Curate Anesko's room and Maren opened the door to the hidden room. It was about the same size as the first one, but we weren't forced to sit down to see into the Curate's chambers. After an hour of sitting idly, Anesko entered the room and sat at his desk. He flipped through a stack of books and scattered parchments around as he scratched notes. I assumed he was studying or something, but he certainly wasn't doing anything suspicious.

The small room was warm and cozy. I must have dozed off, because the next thing I knew, Maren was jabbing me with her elbow.

"What is it?" I asked. I saw that Anesko was gone.

"You were snoring," she complained. "You're

lucky Anesko left before you got too loud."

"Sorry," I said, shrugging.

"Let's get out of here before he comes back."

We left and navigated our way through the maze of hallways until we reached an area I didn't recognize.

"Where are we?" I asked.

"This is the hall for female Curates," Maren said. "The chambers are on opposite sides of the Citadel."

Maren paused outside the first door on the left side of the hall.

"Whose room is this?" I asked.

"Curate Josphine's."

After having listened to the council meeting earlier, I didn't think Josephine would be a spy. She was too nice to be evil. I didn't bother voicing my opinion to Maren. She would refuse to listen until she saw it for herself. Maren knocked gently on the door. There was no answer. She waited a moment, then pushed the door open. Its hinges creaked softly.

I let Maren go in first. She looked around and waved me in. Josephine's room was much different than Anesko's. There were no windows and no candles. Instead, a ball of light hovered near the ceiling. It bobbed up and down a few inches, causing shadows to flutter back and forth across the room.

"This is …" Maren paused.

"Different?" I offered.

"I was going to say creepy."

I rolled my eyes. It was a *little* creepy, but I wouldn't tell her that. "Is there another one of those hidden rooms in here?"

Maren smiled at me and walked over to the wall beside a tall bookcase. She pushed on one of the bricks in the wall and it slid to the side. My eyes widened in shock. Inside the small chamber was an elderly woman. I didn't know who she was. Maren gasped.

The woman was bound and gagged. Her eyes were closed and for a moment, I thought she was dead. Upon further inspection, her body moved with her breathing and relief washed over me.

"I think we know who's working for the False King," Maren said, looking at me from over her shoulder.

"We need to move her out of here," I replied. "Before Josephine comes back."

Just as we stepped into the small room, I heard footsteps echoing in the hallway. Fear made my heart feel like it dropped into my stomach. Maren closed the door and we sat in the dark, not daring to move at all. I watched through the bricks, which I was beginning to suspect were enchanted, as Josephine walked into the chamber. She closed the door and locked it. The Curate walked with a natural grace that I hadn't noticed before.

In the center of the room was a brazier that looked like it had never been used. It was made of steel and shined eerily under the magical light. Josephine walked over to it and drew a dagger from her robes, then ran the edge of the blade across her palm. I winced involuntarily.

Josephine knelt in front of the brazier and ran her bloody hand across the middle of it. I knew that she was probably about to cast a spell, and my curiosity kept my eyes glued to her. She grabbed a handful of bright yellow powder from a bowl beside the brazier and spoke an arcane word as she threw the powder onto the brazier.

Flames roared to life and the smell of smoke and ether filled my nostrils. I glanced over at Maren, but she was watching Josephine as intently as I was.

"Master," Josephine said.

I turned my gaze back to the Curate. A dark figured appeared in the brazier. The figure was wearing a robe and reminded me of the man who had battled the boy in my Compassion test. Dread started to set in as I realized that the two could be connected if not the same man entirely.

"What is it?" the figure asked. His voice was the same, hollow and shrill.

"We have a problem."

The figure turned completely around in the brazier, taking in the surroundings.

"Are we alone?"

"Yes. Mostly."

"Mostly?"

"One of the kitchen workers saw me putting poison into the food for Master Pevus," Josephine said. "I was forced to tie her up and she is here with us now."

"A servant?" the figure asked.

"Yes, Master."

The magical ball of light flickered.

"Why do you waste my time with such trivial matters? Kill the servant and finish your task."

"Kill her? Are you sure?"

The room darkened even further until I could barely see Josephine's outline.

"Forgive me, Master," Josephine whispered. I could hear the fear in her voice.

"Forgiveness is for the weak," the figure said. "Do as I have commanded, or I will send another to replace you."

"Of course, Master."

"Is there anything else?"

"Master Pevus is growing suspicious," Josephine replied. "One of the students was warned of the False King's return by the magic of the testing chamber."

"I'm aware of the magic's warning," the figure said dismissively. I knew then that the figure from my test and the one speaking were the same.

"Master Pevus has dispatched scouts to the border. They should arrive soon."

"Yes, they arrived a few hours ago. Master Pevus should not expect their return."

Maren and I looked at each other at the same time. I could see my concern reflected in her green eyes. My heart was pounding and sweat droplets were rolling down my sides. This was bad.

"Won't that make him more intent on finding out what's happening?"

"Let him wonder. My army swells in number daily. By the time the dragoons are recalled across the kingdom and reach the border, it will be too late. I have other matters to attend to. Kill the servant and poison Master Pevus. Do not fail me in this."

Josephine bowed. The light brightened and the dark figure faded from view. The brazier was spotless as if there had been no blood on it at all. The silence was intense and I held my breath for fear that Josephine would hear me. She rose and stepped toward us, then hesitated. She had a thoughtful look on her face, then she unlocked the door and left.

I waited a moment to make sure she was gone before pushing the wall open and stepping out. Maren joined me and we looked at the bound woman.

"This is the proof we need," Maren said. "If we can get her to the master, she can tell him what she saw."

"I can't believe Josephine is the spy," I said.

"You heard and saw what I did," Maren replied. "Hurry, let's carry her to the master's chamber."

Maren grabbed the woman's feet and I tried to lift her by the shoulders, but she was heavier than she looked.

"She's frail," I said. "How is she so heavy?"

Maren closed her eyes and whispered something under her breath. A few seconds later, she opened them and said, "It's magic. I can sense it."

"Can you break the spell?" I asked.

"No. It's powerful magic. Old magic."

"What do we do? We can't just leave her here." I said.

"We'll have to. Just long enough to get the master and bring him back here."

Without another word, we ran to Master Pevus's chamber.

14

Master Pevus listened to Maren's tale without saying a word.

His face, however, became stern as she talked. I was ready for him to call for dragoons to find Josephine and lock her in the dungeon. Instead, he surprised me.

"You are walking a dangerous line," Master Pevus said. "Accusing a Curate of treachery and potential murder without proof will have you removed from the school, regardless of who you are."

"We *have* proof," Maren said. "The woman is still in Josephine's chamber. She's been ensorcelled in place. We tried to move her before I realized that a spell was preventing us from doing so."

"Master," I said. "I was there and saw everything Maren told you. Two witnesses must account for something."

"Very well," Master Pevus said, rising from his chair. "Lead the way."

Maren took off straight away. I followed after her and Master Pevus brought up the rear. I was worried that he might not be able to keep up, but after a couple of glances over my shoulder, I had nothing to worry about. Although he was aged, he moved quickly and stayed close behind me.

The entire way, I hoped that we hadn't taken too long. If the woman had been killed, I didn't know what I would do. I silently prayed that the woman was safe. As we neared the door to Josephine's chamber, Master Pevus strode past us and pushed it open. He disappeared inside and Maren and I hurried to catch up.

"I see nothing," Master Pevus said, looking around the room.

Everything was the same except the hidden chamber was now closed. Maren walked over to the wall and pushed the same brick as before, then stood aside as the wall slid open. Master Pevus seemed taken aback. I looked inside and saw that the woman was gone.

"How do you know of the hidden room?" he asked.

"I saw it on a map," Maren replied. "But look!" She pointed and turned to look inside the room. Then she froze.

"Look at what?" Master Pevus demanded.

"The woman was in here," Maren said. "She was lying right here!"

Master Pevus looked at me and I nodded. "She was."

He looked back at the hidden room and remained silent for so long that it became uncomfortable. I had no idea what he was thinking. My thoughts were on the woman. Where had she gone? Had Josephine carried her off to kill her in someplace less conspicuous? My heart sank in defeat. We were too late.

"You will not repeat what you told me to anyone," Master Pevus said. "Is that clear?"

"Yes, Master," I said.

"Do you believe us?" Maren asked.

"How can I? There is nothing here to suggest your story ever happened."

"Why would we lie about it?" Maren said, indignant.

"Why indeed? Regardless, you will not tell this story to anyone and I will not excommunicate you from the school for false claims. This behavior is very unbecoming of a princess."

Maren opened her mouth as if to say something, but Master Pevus scowled and she remained quiet. We left Josephine's room and Master Pevus closed the door and offered us each a pointed look, then he stalked off.

After he was gone, I looked at Maren questioningly. "A princess? You're a *princess? The princess?*"

Maren rolled her eyes. "Yes, but that doesn't matter."

"Yes, it does matter. Why didn't you tell me? And how're you royalty? Your hair is black."

Maren grabbed some of her hair and ran her fingers through it, making them black. Where she had rubbed, her hair was red. I stared in disbelief.

"What is that stuff?" I asked.

"Charcoal."

"Why are you hiding who you are?"

Maren sighed and cast her gaze to the floor. "You wouldn't understand."

"I might."

"All my life, I've been given whatever I want simply because of who I am."

"Is that a complaint?" I asked, not trying to hide the sarcasm.

"What I mean is that I never have to work for anything. I never have the opportunity to prove myself. I thought if I came here and passed the tests with no one knowing who I was, then I would finally show everyone, and myself, what I can do."

That made sense to me. I found it difficult to understand why someone would want to step away from having everything to willingly work for something, but I could understand her intent. I, too, wanted to prove that I was worthy to be a dragoon, to prove that I was worthy of the respect that my father's deeds had earned.

"You could have told me," I said. "Are you really a sorcerer?"

"Yes," Maren replied. "Why?"

"Well, I don't know what to believe when it comes to you. No wonder you weren't scared of being kicked out of the school for breaking the rules. Your father would just force Master Pevus into letting you stay."

"That's not true. My father may be the king, but he doesn't have any authority here."

"Based on what we heard in the council meeting, *that* may not be true," I replied.

Maren paused. She knew I was right. The king could demand anything he wanted, from anyone.

"It doesn't matter," I said. "We need to find where Josephine took that woman."

"I don't even know where to start," Maren said. "I don't know anything about Josephine, so it's going to be difficult tracking down where she goes."

"Are you giving up?" I asked.

"No, of course not. I never give up."

"Then let's start looking."

We left Josephine's room behind and searched for hours. Everywhere we looked, there was no sign of Josephine or the elderly woman. Maren led me to tons of hidden rooms. All of them were empty and didn't appear to have been used in years. Thick layers of dust covered the floors and the only prints that marred the dust belonged to mice. Or rats.

The thirteenth bell rang, signaling dinner. Neither of us admitted what we feared, but I knew that she had the same thoughts I did. Josephine had probably killed the old woman already. If we could at least find the body, then perhaps that would be enough proof for Master Pevus. We headed to the dining hall in silence.

I ate until I was full, but I could barely taste the food. Everything from earlier felt like a dream, as though it hadn't happened. As much as I wished that was true, I knew that Josephine was an agent of the False King.

"Who do you think that man is that Josephine was talking to?" I asked.

"I don't know," Maren replied. "He gives me the creeps, though."

"Same here. He was able to control Josephine's magic ball of light, so he must be a sorcerer of some kind."

"That makes sense, but I only know of a handful of sorcerers who aided the False King in his war, and they all died."

"Did they?" I asked. "Everyone seems to think the False King died as well, but recent events make it sound like that may not be the case."

"Fair enough," Maren said.

I yawned and leaned back in my chair. "We only have a few hours before curfew. I want to keep searching, but I'm exhausted and tomorrow we have to take the next test."

Maren looked at me. Her eyes were watery.

"What's wrong?" I asked.

"I can't help but think that I could have done more to free that woman from Josephine's spells."

"You said yourself that the magic was too strong."

"I know, but I didn't even try to break the spell. What if I had and we had been able to free her? She would still be alive."

"She could still be alive now," I said. "We haven't found any trace of them, but that doesn't mean Josephine killed her. Maybe she just moved her somewhere else?"

"Maybe," Maren replied. She wiped the edges of her eyes with the end of her sleeve.

"We can look some more tomorrow when our tests are done," I offered.

"That's a good idea. I think I'm going to bed early," Maren said. "I've got a lot on my mind that I need to deal with."

"Now that is a good idea," I said.

"That's the only kind I have," Maren said, her mouth curling into a smirk.

"There she is." I didn't like seeing her downcast, but I understood how she felt. If we had done more to try and free the woman, perhaps we would have succeeded. We left the dining hall and walked together to our wing of the Citadel. Halfway there, Maren grabbed onto my hand and held it until we parted ways at the top of the stairs.

"Goodnight, Eldwin. And good luck tomorrow. I'll meet you here after the tests?"

It was a question more than a statement, and I

nodded. "Yes, it's a plan."

"Good." She started to walk away, then paused. "It could be a date, instead."

Then she left me standing alone, my cheeks flushed red.

15

When the bell rang for breakfast in the morning, I was already awake and dressed in my robes. I'd found it difficult to get to sleep after Maren had said our time today would be a date. Who would have thought that a low born like me would even spend time with a princess, let alone go on a *date* with one?

Certainly not me.

I entered the dining hall and filled my plate with a biscuit and some eggs. Steam rose from the eggs and the smell made my mouth water. I had noticed that most of the other students didn't come in for breakfast until later. The lack of chores had probably made them more apt to sleep in. Since today was the second test, I made sure to eat enough to hold me over until lunch.

Oddly, I didn't see Maren. After I finished eating, I wandered the halls for a while to see if I could find her, but I had no luck. I ended up going back to our wing of the Citadel to wait for Curate Anesko. He was already there, and he didn't look happy. I heard him muttering about everyone running late. I was glad to be one of the only ones waiting. Maybe he would look on me favorably for being early.

As everyone else slowly joined us, I saw Maren coming from the direction of the stables and realized why I hadn't found her. I shook my head at her and she flashed me a smile. No one could keep her away from the dragons. She came to stand beside me.

"Begging for trouble?" I whispered.

"You're just jealous," she said with a laugh.

"Seriously, Maren. I would try to keep away from trouble. Especially since Master Pevus didn't believe us about …" I glanced around to make sure no one was listening. "… you know who."

"I won't get caught," she said.

I stared at her until she offered an exaggerated sigh. "Fine. I suppose you're right."

Curate Anesko cleared his throat, drawing our attention. The group went silent.

"Today you will all be taking the Magical Aptitude test. This test will evaluate your common sense when it comes to spellcasting. Unlike the Compassion test, this one is much more involved and will likely go late into the evening."

Anesko paused and looked at each of us in turn. I was trying to figure out how I would take a test that required magical talent when I didn't have any. I was fairly certain that none of us, except for Maren, had any magical inclination.

"Those of you lucky enough to bond with a dragon will learn many things. One of which is that dragons are powerful magic users. As the bond grows, you will gain abilities you don't currently have. Most of you will gain the skill to cast minor spells, but some of you may become strong in spellcasting, especially depending upon your dragon.

"If you do not currently possess the talent for magic, you will be given a potion that will temporarily allow you to cast spells. You will drink it before entering the test and it will last for several hours. That should be plenty of time to get through the obstacles. If not, then you will know that you failed. Are there any questions?"

Silence.

"Good. Follow me."

Curate Anesko led us out of the Citadel and to the right side of the grounds. We were still behind the wall that separated the school from the surrounding city. Large, towering bushes formed a solid wall that I was unable to see through. The bushes seemed out of place as if they weren't normally there.

A long table was set up nearby, covered with at least a hundred vials filled with green liquid. In front of the table, rows of chairs had been set out. Anesko ordered us to sit and we obeyed. The wall of shrubbery rippled oddly, like a wave across the surface of a lake, and then it split open and Master Pevus stepped out. I craned my neck to glance into the opening and briefly saw a maze before the wall closed.

The Master still looked rough, but he didn't seem as exhausted as yesterday. The Curates gathered around him and they conversed lowly. I assumed they were talking about the test or something related to it. I smiled at Maren as she sat beside me.

"Are you nervous?" she asked.

"A little," I lied. I was terrified, more so than I was for the Compassion test. Even though we would drink a potion that would let us use magic, I knew nothing about the arcane and feared I was going to fail.

"Don't be. You'll do fine, I'm sure. You've got a strong will. And spellcasting is mostly impressing your will on the magic to do what you want it to."

"Really?" I asked.

"Yes. For me, it helps if I close my eyes and try to visualize what I want the magic to do. Sometimes, anger makes the spell stronger."

"Like in the alley?"

Maren nodded. We watched as Master Pevus called the first student up. Curate Anesko handed the student a vial from the table. He drank it, then walked toward the wall of bushes. They parted to let him enter, then quickly closed once he walked inside.

The next few hours were filled with excruciating boredom as we waited. Lunch was catered outside, and no one was allowed back into the Citadel unless they needed to use the lavatory. And that required an escort from one of the Curates.

The sky was overcast and a gentle breeze was blowing, which provided a respite from the heat. It was the middle of summer, and days like this were rare, so I enjoyed every minute of it. I leaned back in my chair and closed my eyes. The wind felt amazing against my face. I tried to imagine what the wind would feel like while riding on the back of a dragon.

Eventually, I opened my eyes and became aware of dragons flying overhead. There were two of them. One was blue, and the other was green. They floated lazily above the maze, and I assumed their riders were looking down, watching the test unfold. The scales of the dragons shimmered and I nudged Maren with my elbow.

"Look," I said.

She looked up and smiled. "I think that's Azer and Zymon."

"They have names?" I asked. It sounded dumb as soon as the words left my mouth.

"Of course. All dragons have names."

"How do you know their names?"

"They told me."

"They who?" I asked.

"Azer and Zymon."

"The dragons spoke to you?"

"Sort of," Maren said. "Once you are bonded to one, you'll be able to speak with them telepathically. If you aren't bonded to one, they usually choose to only share impressions with you. Since I've been going down to the stables to see them so often, they've become comfortable around me."

"I would love to do that," I said. "But …"

"You don't want to get in trouble, I know."

I nodded my agreement and continued to watch the dragons as they circled over the maze.

"Do all dragons breathe fire?" I asked.

"Yes, but every color of dragon has a unique breath ability also. Well, almost all of them."

"What do you mean?"

"Blue dragons breathe lightning, but also breathe fire."

"Oh. That's interesting. What about green ones?" I asked.

"Acid. Black dragons also breathe acid."

"White ones?"

"Frost."

That made my brows raise in surprise. "Wow. Imagine a dragon breathing frost at you. You'd probably freeze within seconds."

"Probably," Maren agreed.

"What about red ones?"

"Only fire. They are the exception in that they don't have a second breath, but their fire is much stronger than the other colors."

"What color dragon do you want to bond with?" I asked.

"Green," Maren answered without hesitation. "You?"

"I'm not sure," I said. "I've thought about it a lot, but I just can't decide. I think bonding with any dragon would be amazing."

"I agree."

The hours continued to pass and dinner was also catered outside. By the time the sun began to set, there were still about fifteen students left to be tested, including myself and Maren. When it was Maren's turn to go, she touched my hand briefly, then went up to Master Pevus. Since she was magically inclined, she didn't need to drink one of the vials. I watched her disappear into the maze and began to wonder what awaited me inside.

The sun vanished completely and the Curates cast spells of light to illuminate the area. Glowing balls of light, much like the one I'd seen in Josephine's chamber, bobbed in the air, casting their brilliance everywhere. Except on the wall of bushes. They remained dark as if they sucked the light from the air around them and suffocated it. I swallowed hard as I stared at the wall.

Master Pevus called my name and I rose to my sheet. My knees felt weak and my palms were sweating. *It's time to prove myself,* I thought. *I can do this.*

I reached the table and Curate Anesko gave me

a vial. I held it up and looked at it, then put it to my mouth and lifted the vial. The liquid was thick and sluggish. It felt like an eternity before the bitter taste hit my tongue. I resisted the urge to gag and made sure to drink as much of the stuff as I could. The effect of the potion hit me immediately. It was like I had a sixth sense that had been awakened.

Master Pevus motioned me toward the wall of bushes. "Good luck, Eldwin."

I bowed my head at him as I passed, and stepped in front of the wall. The bushes parted, revealing a dark maze. I could see glowing orbs floating in the maze, similar to the ones the Curates had cast. I cast a final glance behind me, then stepped into the maze.

16

Magic hummed in my ears.

It wasn't overly loud, but it was noticeable. The chirp of crickets, the cries of owls, and many other noises filled the night, but the magic stood out distinctly from every other sound in the maze. I stood still for a moment, taking in the sounds and looking around. The walls of the maze were all formed of the same shrubbery. Despite knowing that I was on school grounds and taking a test, I was a little scared.

I looked up to the sky and saw the dark silhouettes of the dragons, faint shapes of blackness against a bigger dark canvas. Somehow, knowing the dragons were up there brought me some comfort. Very few stars were visible, but the moon was full and bright. The pathway I stood on was made of gray and white cobblestones. The white portions glowed faintly under the light of the moon and the magical globes floating around.

"I can do this," I whispered to myself as I took a few steps forward. To my left, there was a brazier filled with flames. An invisible wall of heat washed over me. I was about to walk past it when I felt the pull of magic. It was an urging deep within me, telling me to get closer. Common sense warred against the magic, warning me to keep away. I remembered that Maren told me closing her eyes helped her with spellcasting, so I closed mine and listened to the magic.

Water.

The word formed in my mind. I lifted my hand and imagined a flow of water spraying from my palm. At first, nothing happened. I focused harder, pressing my will against the magic as Maren had told me. There was a slight resistance but it quickly gave way. I felt droplets of water begin to drip from my palm. I opened my eyes in surprise and almost lost the connection to the magic. My sheer stubbornness saved the spell. I refused to let go of the magic.

And then the resistance was gone completely and a torrent of water flowed from my hand. I stared in amazement as the liquid put out the flames in the brazier. The heat faded and I released the magic. I looked at my palm, still reeling from the fact that I had successfully cast a spell. Me. A low born.

I wiped my hand on my robes and looked around, wondering if I was supposed to navigate the entire maze, or just prove that I was magically capable. The wall behind the brazier parted and I felt the pull of magic urging me to go through the opening. I did, and the maze opened up into a large square.

In the right corner, something tall loomed in the darkness. No magical lights shone there, nor did the moonlight seem to be able to penetrate the gloom. Curiosity got the better of me and I walked closer to see what it was. When I was only a few feet away, I felt the ground tremor under my feet. I stopped walking, but it was too late.

The colossal shape in the corner moved toward me. I backpedaled and watched with a horrified interest as the thing, whatever it was, stepped into the light. It was at least three feet taller than me and appeared to be made of dirt and rock. It moved slowly but inexorably drew closer. I kept a decent distance between us, but as I looked around for an escape, I noticed that there wasn't one. The walls had closed and there was nowhere to go.

I kept moving, keeping out of arm's length of the creature, and considered my options. It was possible this was part of the test, but what kind of spell would defeat a creature made of the earth? I didn't know. The magic pulled at me again, subtly getting louder and louder in my conscience until it was like someone was shouting at me—from within my mind. I jogged a few feet further away and closed my eyes for a moment to focus on the magic. Again, a word was impressed upon my mind.

Wind.

What would wind do against such a creature? I opened my eyes and continued moving. The creature didn't stop. It was only a matter of time before I got tired, but this thing could probably walk all night without stopping. I needed to do something.

"Wind," I muttered.

I didn't understand how the wind would stop this creature, but I didn't have any other options. I hurried further away, then turned to face the monster. I closed my eyes and focused on the magic like I had with the first spell and envisioned a whirlwind. I lifted both hands and put all of my willpower into the magic. I could feel the breeze getting stronger, but it was taking too long.

The grumbling sound of the creature was getting closer, but I kept my eyes closed. If I lost the connection to the magic, the creature would have me. I changed plans and instead of a vortex, I imagined a gust of air. The wind picked up and my robes whipped around me frantically.

I opened my eyes just in time to see the giant fist of the creature coming down at me. My eyes widened, but the spell had worked and a powerful gust of wind blew against the creature, pushing it back a few feet. The creature's fist missed me. It roared and struggled to come at me.

Surprisingly, I could feel the creature push against the magic. It was as though the wind were an extension of me, and whatever happened to the wind, I could feel it in some small way. I gritted my teeth and forced the wind to blow harder. The magic obeyed and whirled furiously around the creature. Dirt and pieces of rock began to break free and were pulled away by the wind.

The creature roared again. It moved around, trying to escape, but the wind was destroying the creature bit by bit. With a sudden gust, the creature's head parted from its body and the rest of it collapsed into a mound of rubble. I commanded the magic to stop and the wind calmed. I was overcome with exhaustion and almost fell over. My vision blurred and I thought I was going to pass out.

After a few moments of panic, the weakness went away but I still felt drained. Was the magic tied to my strength? If so, that could end up being very inconvenient. The wall of shrubbery directly across from where I came in shifted and opened up. I walked through and found myself on a long, straight path. The walls rose up on either side of me, dark and imposing. I stepped slowly and quietly, not wanting to be surprised again.

I got midway along the path when I noticed a gray statue. It was in the wall of shrubbery to my right. The ornate details were startling, and for a moment I thought the statue was alive. I stared at it for a long while, then continued down the path. A sound behind me made me stop. I didn't turn around, but I listened intently.

Nothing.

I looked over my shoulder, but there was nothing there. And then I saw that the statue was gone. My heart started pounding in my chest and I realized that the statue might be alive after all. I turned back and there it was in front of me. It had wickedly sharp teeth and long, deadly claws. The magic felt different now. It wasn't pulling me ahead, but urging me to flee. Why would the magic tell me to run from the test?

The statue hissed and clawed at me, ripping the sleeve of my robe. Thankfully, it didn't scratch my skin. I leaped backward and tried to force the magic to fling the statue away with a gust of wind, but I couldn't quite latch onto the magic. It was like trying to grab ahold of a slippery fish. The statue creaked as it jumped into the air, stone wings giving it flight. In horror, I realized it wasn't just a statue.

It was a gargoyle.

Any idea of fighting was quickly banished from my mind and I turned and fled back the way I'd come. The wall was still open, and I ran through it and back into the large square. The gargoyle was right behind me. I threw myself to the ground and the beast flew narrowly overhead, its claws swiping at me.

This wasn't part of the test. It couldn't be. There was no way that Master Pevus nor the Curates would have allowed such a dangerous creature to be part of the test. A gargoyle was all but undefeatable by someone like me.

"Help!" I screamed.

The gargoyle whipped around in the air and came flying back at me. I scrambled to my feet and tried to get out of the way, but the stone creature struck me squarely in the side and I tumbled to the ground with a cry of pain. My ribs were on fire and I was afraid that some of them might be broken.

The gargoyle stood over me. It flashed a smile at me and then spoke in a gravelly voice.

"You … die … now."

I closed my eyes, not wanting to see what the creature was going to do. There was a fluttering sound, followed by a cracking noise, and I opened my eyes to see a dragon and its rider. The dragon had the gargoyle in its powerful claws and had snapped it into pieces. The dragon tossed the remainder of the gargoyle's body aside and gazed down at me, its intelligent eyes looking me over.

The rider leaped down from the saddle and knelt beside me. "Are you all right?"

"Yes," I said. "Thank you. If you hadn't come just now, I'm sure I'd be dead right now."

"It was a close call, but Azer spotted the danger before you cried out. Dragons have exceptional eyesight, even in the dark, so your thanks belong to her."

I looked at the massive blue dragon. "Thank you."

The dragon tilted its head, almost like a human nod.

"Come on," the rider said. "Let's get you out of here. Master Pevus will want to know how a gargoyle got into the testing grounds, I'm sure."

The rider helped me to my feet and then climbed into the saddle. I scrambled up the side of the dragon and sat behind the rider. With a powerful flex of its wings, the dragon lifted into the air. I looked down at the gargoyle's broken body and couldn't help but wonder if Josephine was behind the attack.

17

I was sitting in a small room outside Master Pevus's office, listening to hushed voices.

The dragoon who had come to my rescue sat across from me, dozing in and out of sleep. After landing outside of the maze, the dragoon had informed Master Pevus what had happened and the remaining tests were put on hold while the Curates investigated the maze. Once the Curates had confirmed there were no other hidden dangers, the tests resumed and Master Pevus ordered the dragoon and me to follow him. A quick check by a healer confirmed my ribs were *not* broken, despite the throbbing.

I feared that I would have to retake my test or, worse, that I failed since I had called for help. The dragoon had said that the gargoyle wasn't supposed to be there, so that did ease my fear a little. I thought about Maren and wondered if she had heard what transpired. Master Pevus's door opened and Curate Anesko stepped out and left.

"Eldwin," Master Pevus's voice echoed into the room. "Please, come in."

I rose from my chair and went stepped through the doorway. I'd yet to see the Master's office and was surprised to find that it was sparsely decorated. There was a desk, which Master Pevus was sitting behind, and a couple of chairs. There were no paintings or anything else to show that the office was used by anyone.

"Are you all right?" he asked.

"Yes, Master. A little shaken up, I suppose, but I wasn't injured too badly. My robes were torn, though."

"Good, good. We'll get you another pair. I want to apologize to you. That creature wasn't part of the test, nor should it have been there at all. The maze is protected by powerful spells to keep such things from happening, yet here we find ourselves. The Curates checked the spells and they are all intact. That leaves only one explanation."

I waited for him to continue. He rubbed his eyes and leaned forward, folding his arms and placing them on the desk.

"Someone put the gargoyle there or allowed it to enter."

Was he thinking the same thing I was? That Josephine was behind it?

"When you and Maren told me about your suspicions regarding Josephine, I didn't believe it. Not at first. Some things are happening that I cannot tell you, but I will say that as I considered your allegations, certain things did seem to fall into place. You and Maren are right about Josephine."

I felt a rush of relief. "Thank you, Master. We weren't lying."

"I see that now. I trust you understand why I

wouldn't believe a claim like that about one of the Curates?"

"Of course," I replied. "I didn't want to believe it myself."

"To make a long tale short, I placed Josephine under Curate Anesko's watchful eye. He has confirmed that she is spying on us for someone, but we don't know who."

"Maren said it was the False King," I said. "but the man Josephine spoke with was someone different."

"Yes, that man is also a servant of the False King, but we don't know his identity yet."

"I thought he was dead? The False King, I mean."

Master Pevus sighed. "So did I. It seems that may not be the case after all."

"What does that mean?" I asked.

"It means dark times are ahead. The False King came very close to achieving his ambitions in the last war. I'm afraid we've grown lax in our watchfulness, and it will be difficult to defeat him a second time."

Master Pevus must have noticed my facial expression, for he waved his hands and stood up.

"Please, don't think about such things. The Curates and I are already in communication with the king and his advisors. We will sort things out and deal with the False King. Now, you should get some rest. Due to all of these things and more, we cannot delay the testing any further. Tomorrow, we will conclude the testing and make our decisions."

We left the office and Master Pevus kicked a leg of the chair the dragoon was sitting in, causing him to startle awake.

"Apologies, Master," he said, standing. "It's been a long shift."

"I understand," Master Pevus said, offering a smile. "You are dismissed. Report back to your commander."

The dragoon bowed and hurried away.

"As for you, know that your father would be proud of how you've handled the tests so far."

"Thank you," I said. "I only wish he were here to see it for himself."

"Indeed."

I started to leave, then paused and turned to look at Master Pevus.

"I have a question. Curate Anesko said that the tests would be so hard it would make us wish we were dead. The Magical Aptitude test didn't seem that difficult, so why would he say that?"

Master Pevus tried to keep from smiling but failed. "Curate Anesko likes to exaggerate to weed out any potentials that might doubt themselves."

"That makes sense," I said.

"However, you did much better with magic than

most everyone else in your class. So, while it may have seemed easy to you, it was not for many others."

Excitement welled within me. His words meant I passed! At least, that's how I perceived them. Either way, the fact that I had handled the magic so well could only mean good things in the future.

"Don't repeat what we've spoken about to anyone," Master Pevus said.

"I won't. Goodnight, Master."

"Goodnight, Eldwin."

I navigated my way back to my room and realized it was well after midnight when I climbed into my bed. I drifted off to sleep almost immediately.

When I awoke, one of the bells was ringing. I didn't know which one it was, so I jumped up to get ready. I noticed a new robe was folded and set at the edge of my bed. I switched it for the torn one I had fallen asleep in and hurried down to the dining hall. It turned out it was the third bell, signaling breakfast.

I ate quickly and headed back to my wing to await Curate Anesko. Maren was already there. I stood beside her and gave her a tired smile.

"Late night?" she asked.

"Too late," I replied. "Did you hear what happened?"

"Bits and pieces. The Curates were squashing

any rumors."

"A gargoyle attacked me during the test."

"So, that *did* happen? Wow. You're lucky to be alive."

"Tell me about it," I said. "Azer saved my life."

"She's a good dragon," Maren said. "I like her. It's too bad she's already bonded, or I'd love to pick her."

I leaned in close to her and whispered, "Master Pevus said he knows we weren't lying about Josephine."

"Really?" she asked eagerly.

"Yes. He had Anesko watch her and he confirmed the same thing."

"Well, I heard she hasn't been seen in the last few hours. Dragoons were sent to arrest her. They checked her room, but she's nowhere to be found."

"Maybe she fled the school?" I said.

"I don't think so."

"Where else would she be?"

"I'm not sure, but I plan on looking for her today."

"We have our last test today," I said.

"I know. I'm going to sneak off and come back before it's my turn."

"Maren." I stared at her. "You won't know when it's your turn. You're likely to be late and then …" I trailed off when I saw the hardness in her eyes. She'd already made her decision.

"I'm not asking you to come with me," Maren said. "I only want to look around and see if I can find any sign of where she's gone, then I'll let Master Pevus know."

"What about our date?" I asked, changing the subject.

Maren laughed. "Did you think I forgot? Just because it didn't happen yesterday doesn't mean it won't happen at all."

"Fair enough," I replied.

Curate Anesko joined our group. For the first time since I'd been here, he looked tired. His eyes had small puffy bags under them and he stifled a yawn.

"Today is the final test. If you are still here, you've passed the first two. You'll notice that some of you are missing. They've failed and been excused from the school."

I looked around. Anesko wasn't lying. At least a third of our group was absent. I exchanged glances with Maren.

"Strength and Arms. That is what today's test will entail. If you want to be a dragon rider, you must prove you have the strength and that you are capable with a weapon. There will be several parts to this test, including armed combat against another student. Today will determine if you will be here tomorrow. Prepare yourselves for what's to come.

Follow me."

We followed Anesko out of the school and to the opposite side of the Citadel we'd been on yesterday. Master Pevus and the other Curates were there waiting. I wondered how Master Pevus was able to function off so little sleep, but I guessed he must be used to it.

Tree branches, all thick and heavy looking, were set in a pile. As soon as we had gathered around it, Master Pevus pointed at the branches and said, "Grab one and take a lap around the city of Autumnwick."

I looked at Maren in uncertainty. She shrugged. That sounded easy compared to everything else we'd been through. None of us moved, obviously waiting for the rest of his instructions.

"Well, what are you waiting for? Go!"

I rushed forward and grabbed a branch and hefted it onto my shoulders, then ran for the gate that led to the city. The branch was heavier than it looked, and my muscles were already crying out in protest.

Perhaps this wouldn't be as easy as I thought.

18

By the time I'd made it around the entire city and arrived back at the Citadel, I was ready to collapse from exhaustion. The lack of sleep from the night before wasn't helping either.

Maren jogged in shortly after me, and her face was flushed red. A layer of sweat glistened on her forehead. She dropped the branch and bent forward, placing her hands on her knees and heaved in deep breathes. I retrieved a water skin and brought it to her.

"Thank you," she huffed. She drank deeply and handed the skin back to me.

"You all right?" I asked.

"I'm fine," she replied. "Just didn't expect that first thing in the morning."

"Tell me about it," I said.

"What are you stopping for?" Curate Anesko said. "The next obstacle is ahead." He pointed to a wooden wall that had been erected with ropes hanging down from the top of it. "Climb without using your legs!"

I gawked at Anesko, but if he saw my look, he ignored it. I shook my head in disbelief and ran over to the wall and grabbed onto one of the ropes. My mangled hand could grip the rope, but I wasn't sure if my arm had the strength to lift my bodyweight that far. The wall was at least three times my height.

"You can do this," Maren said from beside me.

Her encouraging words lit a fire inside me and I began pulling myself up with only my arms. To say it was the hardest thing I'd ever done was an understatement. I kept sliding down and burning my hands on the rope. For every foot I gained, I lost two. A frustrated glance around me showed everyone was struggling, but not nearly as bad as I was.

My hands were blistered raw and bleeding, and my arms were burning intensely. I hung in place and my arms were shaking so much I thought about just giving up. And then I reminded myself that if I failed, I had nothing. I heaved in a deep breath and then pushed myself further than I thought possible and struggled up the rope. I was the last one to reach the top, but I made it.

I scrambled down the other side and followed after the others. One of the Curates was directing us into a long trench filled with mud. Since I was last in line, I was able to see that it was deep enough that it would reach my chest. When it was my turn, I leaped into the trench, splashing into the mud. It quickly became obvious that it was difficult to move through. I was so exhausted I wasn't sure if I would make it to the end before I passed out.

Everything became a desperate blur and the next thing I knew I was lying at the other end of the trench staring into the sky. My robes were caked with mud and weighed heavily on me. All I wanted to do was close my eyes and sleep. Maren's face appeared above me and she offered her hand. I clasped her wrist and she pulled me to my feet.

"Is it over yet?" I asked.

"Not even close," Maren replied. "But it sounds like this was the hardest portion. Next are some exercises with weapons."

"That's great to hear. I can do weapons."

We walked together to where Master Pevus and the Curates were waiting. The other students were gathered around them in a circle, some kneeling and others lying on the ground.

"Everyone has done well so far, but now the easy work is over," Curate Anesko said. Master Pevus tried to hide his grin, but I saw it and remembered his words from the night before.

"The remainder of the day will consist of armed combat. You will each be paired with a senior student. Real weapons will be employed, but we have healers standing by in the event anyone is grievously wounded."

Anesko turned full circle slowly, looking at everyone that remained.

"Let me say this: if you are injured to the point a healer is needed, you have failed. We don't expect you to beat your opponent, as most of you likely won't, but we do expect you to hold your own in a fight and show that you're able to handle a weapon without chopping your leg off. If anyone has any hesitation about their abilities, please speak up now."

I watched those near me to see if anyone was going to forfeit the last test, but no one did. A makeshift arena had been set up, with a circular enclosure for the combatants to fight inside and seating around it for everyone to watch. Knowing that everyone would be watching me fight made me a little uneasy, but I supposed everyone felt that way.

The matches started much like the other tests. A student was called by name and told what to do, then outfitted in a chainmail shirt and given a sword of their choice from a small rack. The idea of using my father's sword was great, but I doubted they would allow me that privilege. I took a seat next to Maren and watched as the first student walked into the enclosure.

The senior student he was up against was also wearing a chainmail shirt and held his sword with practiced ease. One of the Curates rang a bell and the two combatants circled each other, offering a jab here and there to test one another's defenses. I began formulating tactics for how I hoped my test would go. After a few more circles around each other, the two clashed in a heated battle.

I watched every move of the senior student intently, curious to know his style and compare it to the other senior students as the matches continued. I wanted to have an edge over my fellows and possibly win my match. As the senior student whirled around and slashed his blade across the chest of his opponent, I realized that it was highly unlikely I would be able to win. If it weren't for the chainmail shirt, the student would have received a deep life-threatening gash in his chest.

"The opponents we face are probably going to make us look like children with sticks," I said to Maren.

"I learned how to defend myself from the captain of my father's guard," Maren replied. "I'm sure I can hold my own. How long do you think each match will take?"

I shrugged. "If they all go like this one, probably not long. Why?"

Maren looked toward the gate that led to the city and I suspected I knew what she was thinking. She looked back at me and frowned.

"I have a feeling that Josephine is still here," she said.

"I'm sure she is, but you promised to stay out of trouble."

"I know, but …" Maren looked toward the city again. "There's something I can't explain that's telling me I need to find her. I think the elderly woman is still alive."

I bit my lip and considered telling her to go, but I knew that if she were caught leaving or wasn't back in time, her chance at proving herself worthy of being a dragon rider would be gone.

"Just wait until after the test and I'll go with you," I said. "It'll be our date."

Maren didn't reply, but she didn't leave, either. I turned my attention back to the enclosure and watched the next match. It was one of the nobles who'd hung around with Simon. He lasted a little longer than the first student, but he too lost his match.

The next five matches were all the same, but the sixth ended up being a lot bloodier. A student who had probably never touched a sword had his hand cut almost in half. The healers were able to mend it quickly, but the student was shaken and was escorted from the enclosure by one of the Curates.

A portion of the sand inside the enclosure was stained with the student's blood, a reminder that this test was the most physically dangerous. Despite the presence of the healers, I found it almost barbaric to allow such brutality as part of a test to join the school. Then again, those who passed would be trained for combat, riding dragons into battle and probably seeing more brutal things than what this test offered. Still.

"Does your father know what goes on here?" I asked.

"I'm sure he does," Maren replied. "He considers the dragoons to be the most powerful part of his army. He also knows, like everyone else, that becoming a dragoon is far from easy."

"That makes sense," I said.

The next student was preparing to enter the enclosure. So far, there had been a different senior student for each match.

"I wonder how many of these senior students have seen a real battle," I said.

Maren didn't reply, so I turned to look at her.

She was gone.

19

It only took me a moment to decide that I needed to follow her. She couldn't have gotten very far, so I waited until the match started and I was certain Master Pevus and the Curates weren't paying attention to anything except the battling students.

I jogged toward the gate that led to the city, pausing to glance around the grounds of the Citadel. Maren was nowhere to be seen, but I wasn't entirely sure that she had planned to search the city for Josephine. It would make sense that Josephine would hide in the city rather than within the Citadel somewhere, though.

With a final scan of the area, I stepped through the gate and into the city. There were a few empty buildings adjacent to the wall that surrounded the Citadel. They appeared to have once been used for warehouse space. A single smaller building was across from them. I was going to continue further into the city, but I noticed that the side door of the lone building was cracked open.

It could have been nothing relevant, but I decided it was better to check and be sure than to possibly miss something. I walked closer and heard sounds within. There was a muffled cry, then silence. I grew nervous as I got closer to the door. If Josephine and Maren were in there, what help would I be? I wasn't a sorcerer and I didn't know how to fight one, either. But if I ran to get help, it could be too late for Maren.

I swallowed hard and slipped inside the building. There were plenty of windows, but the wall towered high enough that it blocked most of the natural light. It wasn't dark, but it was dim enough that it gave me pause. There was a long corridor with doors on either side, but at the end of the corridor, it opened up into a large room.

My palms were getting sweaty and I wiped them on my robes, which only made things worse because of the mud on the garment. Moving as quietly as I could, I headed for the large room at the end. I heard movement and stopped mid-step. Someone was talking, but it was low and I couldn't make out the words.

I risked a glance and saw all I needed to. The elderly woman that had been bound in Josephine's room was on the floor, curled into a ball. Her eyes were closed, but she was breathing. And next to her was Maren. I ground my teeth in anger.

Maren's arms were bound behind her back and she was sitting on her knees, a roll of cloth in her mouth. Pacing back and forth anxiously was Josephine. I leaned back against the wall, trying to figure out what I should do.

"I can kill them both right now," Josephine said, talking aloud to herself as she paced. "No one will ever find their bodies, but how do I avoid suspicion? *That* is the problem."

By the way she was conversing, it sounded like

she was trying to talk herself into committing the deed. Perhaps she had more of a conscience than I knew. And if she wasn't completely set on the course, maybe I could say something to keep her from hurting them? What could I say, though? I didn't get much time to think about it, because Josephine paced past the opening of the corridor and stopped when she saw me.

Her eyes widened briefly, then she stepped behind Maren, lifted her to her feet, and pressed a wicked-looking dagger to Maren's throat.

"Don't move," Josephine snapped.

I raised my hands in front of me, palms toward her. "I'm not armed," I informed her.

"I don't believe you," Josephine said, narrowing her eyes at me. "Who did you bring with you?"

"Nobody," I replied. "And I'm not lying. I don't have any weapons."

"How did you find me?"

"By accident … but the open door of the building was a good clue."

Josephine scowled and pushed the blade harder against Maren's skin, cutting a small line that bled a little. Anger was boiling within me, but I refused to do anything rash.

"You don't have to do this," I said. "Just let them go."

"You don't understand," Josephine said. "I *must* do this."

"Why? Because that man told you to?"

"What do you know of him?"

"Nothing," I said. "Other than the fact that he radiates evil."

"He is evil. If I don't do this, he'll kill me."

"Not if he can't find you," I said. "Turn yourself into Master Pevus and I'm sure he will help you."

Josephine laughed. It bordered on maniacal and helpless all at once. "Pevus will be dead before long, and he won't be able to help anyone. No, no one can help me. I will do this and prove my loyalty to the Necromancer."

So that's what people called him? I wondered what it meant. If we made it out of this predicament, I was going to ask Maren.

"What for? You murder two innocent people to prove to someone that you are no better than he is? Please, Josephine. Think about this."

"I've thought plenty about this!" Josephine growled. "There is no other way! It's either follow his orders or die."

I felt utterly helpless. My arguments weren't seeming to sway the Curate at all, and she seemed so afraid of the Necromancer that she felt she had no other options. I did the only thing I could do. I begged.

"Please."

Josephine stared at me. I didn't know if sorcerers could read thoughts, but I projected everything I could into my mind that I couldn't put into words and hoped she would understand. Whether or not that's what did it, I didn't know, but she lowered the blade slightly.

"She's your friend," Josephine said.

"Yes."

"And you came here to help her even though you had no way to fight me?"

"Yes," I said again. There was a lump growing in my throat, but I swallowed hard and tried not to let it break my voice, but the tremor was obvious.

The silence stretched into what felt like an eternity. I started to worry that Josephine was going to ignore my plea. Maren was looking at me, so I held her gaze with my own. Whatever happened, at least neither of us was alone.

"Maybe if I had …" Josephine started to say, then trailed off. Her eyes hardened, then they became watery, filling with tears.

"Go," she hissed, pushing Maren toward me. Maren staggered and fell. I slowly knelt and helped her up, keeping my eyes on Josephine. She watched me quietly, but I could still see the turmoil on her face.

"Come with us to Master Pevus," I said.

"Go," she repeated, her tone dangerous.

I nodded and helped Maren to her feet and removed the cloth from her mouth. The elderly woman was still asleep, and when I stepped toward her, Josephine raised the dagger at me. I backed away and grabbed Maren's hand, pulling her with me.

"We have to help the woman," Maren protested.

"We'll come back for her," I whispered. "With Master Pevus."

That seemed to ease Maren's hesitation. We hurried along the corridor to the door. I tried to untie the ropes around Maren's wrists, but it was difficult to do while we were moving. I pushed Maren through the doorway and looked back.

Josephine was still there. She hadn't tried to stop us. The elderly woman was still her prisoner, but I was confident we could reach Master Pevus before Josephine escaped with her. She wouldn't kill the woman. I knew she wouldn't. She was too conflicted with herself to do it. As I was about to close the door, Josephine lifted the dagger. I stopped, too horrified to look away.

The Curate drove the dagger down, into her own chest. I slammed the door closed and cried out, pulling Maren toward the Citadel. I couldn't believe my eyes. Josephine had stabbed herself. Why would she do such a thing?

"What happened?" Maren asked, still struggling to get free of her bonds.

I wanted to tell her, but the words wouldn't come out of my mouth. My throat was constricted tight and it was all I could do to breathe. We made it back to where the others were, and Maren shouted to get someone's attention. Everything became a blur for me. The stress of the day, the physical and mental exhaustion, everything weighed on me and I collapsed near the stands.

Maren screamed. I didn't know if anyone heard her over the commotion of ringing steel. I didn't care. I had experienced death before, but this was something different, something so heavy that I didn't know how I would bear it.

"Are you all right?" I recognized Master Pevus's voice, but it sounded far away. "What happened?"

I pointed toward the way we'd come. "Josephine," I gasped. "She's dead."

20

I didn't know how much time had passed when the storm of emotions finally passed.

Maren had stayed with me almost the entire time, aside from her test, holding my mangled hand and occasionally whispering soft words or making soothing sounds. We sat in the stands and I was vaguely aware of the other students staring at me and whispering to one another.

"Let them wonder," Maren said. "You don't have to tell them anything."

I wouldn't tell them, even if they begged to know. No one needed that knowledge, that pain. Eventually, Master Pevus came to sit with us. The other students finished their testing, but I barely heard any of the noise.

"Death is not an easy thing to witness," Master Pevus said. "Especially a death as tragic as Josephine's."

"I don't understand it," I whispered.

"Neither do I. Not fully."

Master Pevus stared at the enclosure quietly. I started to feel a little more normal, though I was exhausted. Everything felt dreamlike, and for a moment I wondered if any of it had even really happened.

"Do you think you can take the test?" Master

Pevus asked. "I can try to push it back, but the decision is not mine alone."

"What do you mean?" Maren asked.

"The council here at the Citadel is only one of many, and we all report to the Conclave. We have orders that the testing must be completed today, but I can send a letter requesting more time."

"No," I finally spoke. My throat was dry, so it sounded more like a croaking noise. "No," I repeated. "I will take the test."

"Eldwin," Maren said, squeezing my hand. "You need some rest."

"No, I'm fine. I can do it. I *need* to do it."

Master Pevus seemed like he was about to object, but he bowed his head and stood up. "Let us get you ready, then."

I stood up and followed Master Pevus around the enclosure to where the racks of armor and weapons were. Curate Anesko was there and he helped me put a chainmail shirt on. Some of the other students came out of the Citadel and joined Maren in the stands. I didn't know why they wanted to watch my test, but I ignored them. I hoped the test would take my mind off everything else.

Anesko handed me a helm and I slipped it onto my head, then stared at the rack of weapons. There were numerous swords, a few axes, and a single mace. I chose a blade that was closest to the size and heft of my father's sword and nodded at Anesko. He led me into the enclosure and said,

"Good luck. Sebastian is one of the best."

I assumed he was trying to make me second guess myself, so I didn't pay his last comment any attention.

On the other side of the circular battleground was my opponent, Sebastian. It was impossible to tell if I'd seen him before because he was wearing a helm with a visor. I took a few practice swings, stretching my muscles.

This was it. My final test. The defining moment that would determine my future. I took a deep breath and exhaled slowly, then rolled my shoulders and prepared for the bell to ring. A few moments later, the *clang* echoed across the battleground.

I stalked forward slowly, watching Sebastian's posture. He moved with confidence and the ease of a skilled warrior. Perhaps Anesko's comment wasn't entirely exaggerated. We circled one another like giant hunting cats, prepared to pounce at any moment. Sebastian made the first move. He rushed me and swung his sword horizontally, trying to strike me in the chest. I lifted my blade and blocked it.

The blades clanged together loudly. I was surprised at Sebastian's strength and almost lost my grip on the hilt. Although my right arm was shriveled compared to my left, I was right-handed. I'd tried a few times to use my left arm more, but it felt awkward and unnatural.

It quickly became evident as Sebastian struck again and again that my right arm could not hold up under the onslaught. He was keeping me on the defensive, and I knew I had to turn the tide against him somehow. I dropped to one knee as Sebastian swung at me, and it left him open as his sword flew harmlessly above my head.

I jabbed my blade straight into his ribcage. At least, that's where I aimed my strike. Just as quickly as the opening had come, it was gone, and Sebastian had adjusted his stance. The next thing I saw was his thick boot coming straight for my head. I threw myself backward to dodge his foot and slammed hard onto the ground. The force was a little painful, but I ignored it and rolled to the side and scrambled back onto my feet.

Sebastian came at me again, his blade glinting from the sunlight. It flashed brilliantly and I was momentarily blinded. I brought my sword up to try and block the blow I was expecting, but it never came. Instead, pain exploded in my knee and flared up my leg. I cried out in surprise and agony as my leg gave out and I crashed to the ground. I released my hold on the hilt and grabbed my knee.

"Do you need a healer?" Sebastian asked, lifting his visor. His eyes were creased with worry.

I don't know why I did it. Perhaps it was the anger or the exhaustion, but I wasn't in my right mind. I nodded, but it was a lie. I was in pain, but it wasn't as bad as I pretended, and it was quickly fading. As soon as Sebastian turned his back to me, I snatched my sword up and drove it into the back of his legs, right behind his knees. A few of the students in the stands cried out, clearly not liking what they saw.

Red, hot rage flooded my vision and I went to strike Sebastian again, but he crawled out of range on all fours. To his credit, he was still holding onto his blade. I went after him, but he was quicker than I anticipated and got back to his feet and twirled gracefully in a circle, his sword held outstretched. I leaped backward, but the tip of his blade grazed the chainmail that covered my arm.

I was suddenly overcome with guilt for my actions, but there was no time to apologize. It was obvious that I'd angered Sebastian, for he held nothing back. He pressed his attack, his sword a flurry of strikes that I couldn't keep up with. He knocked my sword out of my grasp and landed a solid strike across my chest. Throbbing pain erupted across my flesh despite the armor I wore. Between that and my general exhaustion, I knew I couldn't defeat Sebastian. I collapsed to my knees and put my hands up in surrender.

"Do you yield?" Curate Anesko shouted from outside the enclosure.

"Yes," I tried to shout back, but I didn't know if he heard me.

Sebastian removed his helm, gave me one last long stare, then left the battleground. As I sat there in the dirt, the realization that I had probably failed the test began to set in. Not only had I let my anger get the better of me, but I had also given up. None of it could look good for me.

I slowly got to my feet and returned my armor

and weapon to the racks. Maren joined me as I walked to the Citadel.

"What am I going to do now?" I asked.

"Nothing until you know your results," she replied.

"You know I failed as well as I do. There was no excuse for what I did."

"True, but you did just go through a traumatic ordeal. That has to be taken into account."

Maren had a point, but still. The sinking feeling in my stomach was making me feel like I was going to vomit. Master Pevus said anyone who failed had their memory magically erased so that they didn't remember being at the school or anything they learned. I couldn't allow that to happen. I *wouldn't* allow it to happen.

Maren was talking about her test, but I wasn't listening. I was plotting out how I would escape the Citadel before Master Pevus could erase my memory. There were so many obstacles, though. I had to get past guards, not get caught outside of my room past curfew, and that was assuming they didn't erase my memory without warning.

If this was going to work, I would need help. I looked at Maren and watched her lips move as she spoke. She loved breaking rules, so I had little doubt she'd be willing to help me. She noticed my stare and paused.

"If there something in my teeth?" she asked.

"No," I replied.

"Then why are you staring at me?" she asked.

"I need your help."

"With what?"

I glanced around and lowered my voice. "With breaking into the armory."

21

The next morning, I awoke bleary-eyed and more tired than I had probably ever been in my entire life. Maren and I had been up all night devising my plan of escape and breaking into the armory to retrieve my father's sword.

Maren had left the Citadel and somehow snuck outside the city of Autumnwick to hide my father's sword in a thicket near the lake for me. She said it had been easy and had hidden the weapon so that only I would be able to find it. I assumed she used a spell of some kind. After everything had been planned, we parted ways and went to our rooms. I hadn't slept much, though what little rest I did get had been dreamless.

I was both excited and terrified to find out if I had passed or not. Everything I wanted, everything I was, hinged on my results. I rolled out of bed and put my robes on, then headed down to the dining hall for breakfast. The thought that this could be the last time I knew I'd have a meal was a little disconcerting. It was funny how quickly I had grown accustomed to full meals in the short time I'd been here.

Maren eventually joined me at my table and we ate in silence. I was hoping I'd be able to give her a proper goodbye if I did have to escape the Citadel, but I also knew that might not happen. She had to be aware of that fact as well. I assumed that's why she didn't talk much.

After we ate, we headed back to our normal meeting place to await Curate Anesko. Normally, some of the other students straggled into the group last minute, but today was different. Everyone who remained was on time. There were less than twenty of us. Out of one hundred potentials, only a fifth were left. It was crazy to think I had made it this far only to potentially fail now.

Curate Anesko's footsteps echoed softly off the stone walls as he joined us. His face was solemn, much different than his normal stern appearance. There were bags under his eyes, and I guessed that he had been up late with Master Pevus and the other Curates, deciding the fates of those few students who remained.

"Today some of you will become full students," he said. He swept his gaze over everyone. "And some of you, sadly, will be leaving this place forever."

The word forever sounded so …cold. Barren. Final. But of course, it was. It was all those things and more.

"If I call your name, you will follow me. If I don't, then you will follow Curate Henrik."

One of the students raised a hand.

"Yes?" Anesko asked.

"Are the groups divided into those who passed and those who failed?"

"They are, but if you're expecting me to inform you which group you're in, then you'll be disappointed. Any other questions?"

No one had any. Anesko called out almost everyone's name. Two people weren't called and they left with Curate Henrik. It seemed obvious that the two who weren't called had failed and were being led off to have their memory erased. It seemed surreal that I had passed. Without another word, Anesko led us through the Citadel to the temple where our first test had occurred.

Master Pevus stood beside the temple doors, welcoming every student with a tired smile. Maren and I were at the end of the line, and after Maren stepped through the threshold, Master Pevus stepped in front of me.

"Eldwin," he greeted. "Please, come with me."

My trepidation returned, but mainly because I had no idea why he pulled me aside. Maren looked back at me and I shrugged, then followed Master Pevus's lead. We walked through several of the halls and eventually reached the servant's door that Maren had shown me when we'd secretly went to see the dragons.

"I'm sure you're curious about where we're going," Master Pevus said.

"Yes, Master. It does seem odd to me that we're going out the servant's door," I replied before realizing my error. Master Pevus smiled.

"I see the princess has shown you this door

already."

"Please don't punish her," I said.

"I won't. Besides, it's not a secret door. It's just how the servants come and go."

I breathed a sigh of relief. Master Pevus pushed the door open and we stepped outside. It was still early in the day, and the air was cool. It felt refreshing to be outdoors. My curiosity started to grow as he led me around to the entrance of the dragon stables. The two guards at the entrance were playing dice and quickly stood up when they saw Master Pevus and I approaching.

Master Pevus ignored them and continued walking, leading me deeper into the stables. There were many more torches lit than when I'd been here before, and the details of the cave's carvings were revealed. Long, jagged lines were scraped into the rocks that formed the ceiling, floor, and walls.

"Dragons created this system of caves," Master Pevus said. "Long before the Citadel was ever built. It was a breeding ground, but as humans began to domesticate dragons, they stopped laying their eggs here."

"I've never heard that before," I said.

"This place holds a lot more secrets, though many of them have been lost to the centuries. Tell me, Eldwin. Did your father tell you the color of his dragon?"

"He rode a blue," I said.

"Indeed, he did. Blues are known for their speed, as they are the fastest of all the colors."

We stopped outside one of the caves. A large dragon head appeared as the massive creature moved into the light. It was the same dragon that had spit phlegm on me. The dragon sniffed the air and turned its glowing eyes on me.

"This is Phlandyr," Master Pevus said. "She is a red dragon, though it may be hard to tell in this light."

"Hello Phlandyr," I said.

I felt something press against my mind, but it was faint.

"I thought we weren't allowed near dragons until we were promoted to the rank of Adept?" I asked.

"As a general rule, you're not," Master Pevus confirmed. He went quiet and I stared into Phlandyr's eyes. They were a yellowish hue with black pupils.

"Eldwin, I'm sorry to inform you that you have failed."

"What?" My heart skipped a beat and fell into my stomach.

"You did well in the first test, despite the outside forces that affected it. The second test was interrupted, but not before we were able to see your skill with magic. Yesterday's test, however, showed that you do not handle frustration and failure well.

You allowed your anger to direct your actions. A dragon rider must always have a clear mind, empty of emotions."

"Can I retake the test?" I asked.

"I'm afraid not."

"Please, Master," I begged. My eyes welled with tears. "I can't go home. There's nothing for me there. I have to be a dragon rider."

"I'm sorry, Eldwin. The only way you'll ever ride a dragon is if you find your own."

I felt a tear slip free of my eye. It trailed down my cheek.

"I thought long and hard about this, but I have decided to let you experience what flying on the back of a dragon is like. Your father was a hero, and to honor his memory, I thought this would be fitting."

"Thank you," I said. "But what's the point if you are just going to erase my memory?"

Master Pevus remained silent, but he stepped into the cave and saddled Phlandyr, then led her out of the cave. I walked at his side, trying to figure out a way to escape. My plans with Maren had been based around being locked in a room somewhere, not out in the open on the back of a dragon. Master Pevus mounted Phlandyr and offered me his hand.

I accepted it and climbed into the saddle behind him, then gripped the horn of the saddle tightly. Without any verbal command, Phlandyr leaped into the air and flapped her enormous wings. We climbed higher and higher into the air, the castle below quickly shrinking. Phlandyr banked to the right and she issued a roar.

There were no words to describe the feeling of being on the back of a dragon, flying through the sky. I looked out at the vast landscape that stretched for miles in every direction. Trees that seemed enormous on the ground looked like small sticks, and I could see the entirety of the giant lake that spread out behind the Citadel.

The air whipped around me, pulling at my robes and making my hair ruffle wildly. We flew over the lake and I looked down. Phlandyr dipped lower, flying only a few feet above the water's surface. The lake was crystal clear and I could see fish swimming about. As amazing as the experience was, I knew I was running out of time. Once we landed, the chances of escaping from the Citadel would be slim.

The only way you'll ever ride a dragon is if you find your own.

Those words burned in my mind and I had an idea. It was crazy, foolish even, but I had no other choice. I let go of the saddle horn and swung my right leg over to the same side as my left. Master Pevus tried to turn around to see what I was doing, but he was having trouble. I did a silent countdown, then pushed myself off the side of the dragon just as she bounded upward.

I flipped end over end and saw Master Pevus's

horrified expression before he was too far away to see anymore. I tried to right myself, but I slammed into the water with jarring force. My body screamed in agony and then I was underwater, struggling with which direction was up. I pumped my arms furiously and kicked with my legs until I broke the surface of the water, then I gasped in deep breaths.

Time was my enemy. I turned and swam for the shore as fast as I could. I heard Phlandyr's roars and they drove me to keep swimming even though my muscles wanted to give in. I reached the shore and sprinted to the thicket of trees that Maren had told me about. The air rippled, and then I saw my father's sword. The sheath was attached to a belt and had been hung on a low hanging branch.

I grabbed it and strapped the belt on, then ran in the opposite direction of the Citadel. I had no idea where I was going, but I refused to let Master Pevus erase my memories. He said that the only way I would ride a dragon was to find my own. So be it.

I ran as fast as I could. Away from the Citadel and toward an uncertain future.

I was going to find a dragon of my own.

THE END OF BOOK ONE

ABOUT THE AUTHOR

Richard Fierce is a fantasy and space opera author. He's been writing since childhood, but began publishing in 2007. Since then, he's written multiple novels and short stories.

In 2000, Richard won Poet of the Year for his poem *The Darkness*. He's also one of the creative brains behind the Allatoona Book Festival, a literary event in Acworth, Georgia.

A recovering retail worker, he now works in the tech industry when he's not busy writing.

He's married and has three step-daughters (pray for him), three grandchildren, three dogs (huskies!), a cat, and two ferrets. He basically has a zoo.

His love affair with fantasy was born in high school when a friend's mother gave him a copy of *Dragons of Spring Dawning* by Margaret Weis and Tracy Hickman.